I0680866

Danger

on

Roan Mountain

Saundra Gerrell Kelley

Published by:
Southern Yellow Pine (SYP) Publishing
4351 Natural Bridge Rd.
Tallahassee, FL 32305

All Rights reserved. No part of this publication may be reproduced, stored in a retrieval system, or transmitted in any form or by any means, electronic, mechanical, photocopying, recording, scanning or otherwise, without the prior written permission of the Publisher. For permission or further information contact SYP Publishing, LLC. 4351 Natural Bridge Rd., Tallahassee, FL 32305.

www.syppublishing.com

This is a work of fiction. Names, characters, places, and events that occur either are the products of the author's imagination or are used fictitiously. Any resemblance to actual persons, places, or events is purely coincidental.

The contents and opinions expressed in this book do not necessarily reflect the views and opinions of Southern Yellow Pine Publishing, nor does the mention of brands or trade names constitute endorsement.

ISBN-13: 978-1-59616-112-2
ISBN-13 ePub: 978-1-59616-115-3

LCCN: 2020947449

Copyright © 2020 by Saundra G. Kelley
Front Cover Design: Gina Smith

Printed in the United States of America
First Edition
November 2020

Dedication

In 2006, the mountains of Southern Appalachia in all their beauty welcomed me with open arms. I was there to refine my skills as a storyteller at East Tennessee State University, but those ancient hills gave me much more. Roan Mountain's rhododendron blooms and a blown radiator provided an adventure I will never forget, introducing me to the generosity of the mountain people and in the process, gaining my enduring respect and admiration. They made me feel at home though I would never be native to their sacred ground.

Mimi Jones, Elaine Bartelt, and Jo Anne Jones share this dedication. Their combined love and council at different times in my life taught me to follow my heart, and to write what I know and care about without fear.

Books by Saundra G Kelley

The Day the Mirror Cried
Danger in Blackwater Swamp
Danger on Roan Mountain

Southern Appalachian Storytellers: Interviews with
Sixteen Keepers of the Oral Tradition

Chapter 1

I know it sounds foolhardy, but I dumped my boyfriend and left a dead-end job all in one day. I have no regrets about either.

I had been writing for an eccentric local weekly for two years when Jason Petersen came into my life. One look at him and all thought of leaving the weekly fled my mind. I told myself it was a professional decision, but the truth of it was that I was smitten.

As the paper's new editor-in-chief, he took a flattering interest in my work almost from the beginning, appointing himself as my mentor. Besides his good looks, judging by the awards on his wall, he was a gifted editor and a serious writer, so I was thrilled with the attention.

Together, we investigated and reported on a polluted dump site and then brought a couple of corrupt politicians to justice, so I was definitely interested when he asked me to join him on a water rights leasing project in Wakulla County. An international firm was eying the first-magnitude Wakulla Spring as a source for bottled water, which had the county commission and most of the citizenry in an uproar. Being a naturalist and deeply committed to keeping Florida's rivers flowing clean and free, I signed on and never looked back.

In early December, the air was cooler so we'd spent the first part of the day at the county commission meeting, and then trekked out to the site the company wanted to use to tap into the spring. Hotheaded as always, I threw off my reporter's neutral hat and went ballistic, adamant that the spring and its river should be protected at all costs.

"There's no way the Wakulla Spring should be tapped for bottled water. It's sacred and it belongs to all of us, not some corporation half-a-world away!"

Jason opted for looking at both sides. "Yes, but some of Wakulla County's citizenry think it could bring revenue to a place in need of a little help."

"I know, but think about this. The Wakulla Spring is a part of the Floridan Aquifer—that's where our drinking water comes from!"

While his responses—the yen to my yang—made me furious, it was fun in a way, too. I knew we'd get some good material from the day's research and our banter because we produced some good theories when we argued that way.

At sunset, we declared a temporary truce. Mesmerized, we watched the sky and water turn first to rich golden tones, then to coral, and finally, shades of lavender over Dickerson Bay.

When Mother Earth took Father Sun into her embrace something ignited between us that couldn't be denied. No longer my boss, the man, Jason, turned to me with hot, hungry eyes. I met him halfway, ignoring the seatbelt digging into my neck and the console pressing a dent into my abdomen.

"I don't know about you, but I'm not ready to go home," I whispered between kisses.

"Me either," he said, coming up for air. "Let's go someplace for dinner, someplace close by." He got no argument from me because by that time I had an ache that throbbed for satisfaction.

Considering we were in Wakulla County, which has some very good seafood restaurants, one immediately came to mind that was perfect.

Catching my breath, I said, "Spring Creek Restaurant isn't far from here. Its dining room is cozy, and the food is excellent."

Without a word, my companion turned the car towards the tiny village named for its fresh-water spring. There were other restaurants nearby but I knew exactly what we needed—an intimate atmosphere where we could relax away from prying eyes.

Having met Jason at a church in Medart earlier in the day, I'd left my cypress-green Subaru in the parking lot. It was still there when we passed by, but in the heat of the moment, I gave it little thought.

The drive took about thirty minutes, but I've no memory of it. We pulled into the tiny fishing village of Spring Creek at twilight. Just as I remembered, nestled under fragrant Southern magnolia and moss-draped live oaks stood the rustic Spring Creek restaurant, source of some of the coastal South's best seafood. Barely visible, just to the right and behind the building was the spring for which the village was named—Spring Creek.

Thus, began a magical evening of enchantment and sensual imagery that is forever etched into my memory as one of the most romantic and intoxicating experiences of my life.

It was a weeknight and the small dining room held only two other couples. We sat next to a crackling fire in the limestone fireplace and debated the menu.

"I'm not really hungry," I said, staring down at the entrées. *That's not true*, I told myself. *You're ravenous but not for food.* "I think I'll order fried shrimp with a baked potato and a side salad. What do you want?"

You, his eyes told me, but then he turned to the waiter and said, "I'll have raw oysters for an appetizer and then the fried grouper and shrimp combination. We'll need two wine glasses, please."

I stopped the waiter when he turned away. "Oh, wait, do you still have key lime pie? I want some, but only if it's authentic."

I thought his eyes twinkled at that. "It's as real as you'll ever get, ma'am. My mama makes it the old-fashioned way with fresh key limes she gets shipped up here from South Florida. Makes her own crust and everything. You want me to bring a sample?"

He did, and it was. At any other time, I might have bypassed dinner just to get that taste but this time, it was part of dessert.

The whole time I bantered with the owner's son, Jason ran two fingers up and down my inner arm. It's a wonder I was able to concentrate at all.

After he served our dinners, Jack, our waiter pulled out an old fiddle. He played haunting ballads and love songs while Jason fed me fried shrimp and raw oysters from his own hand, touched my hair, and caressed my arms, almost making love to me with his velvet-brown eyes.

It just so happened the restaurant had a quaint little motel next door.

"I don't want to go home," I told Jason.

"Neither do I. Shall I see if there's a room available?"

At my barely perceptible nod, he rose and went over to Jack while I sipped coffee and tried to contain myself.

We took what was left of the wine and the slice of key lime pie to our room which was at the end of a row of four. That the furnishings were dated had no meaning for either of us; the sheets were clean.

I began to unbutton my blouse. "Let me," he said, and thus began the ancient ritual most of us seem to know by instinct.

When I pulled the blue polo shirt over Jason's head, uncovering the pelt of soft dark hair beneath, I groaned, burying my face in that nest, inhaling his scent. From there we made quick work of it, dropping articles of clothing where they landed.

In that quaint little bedroom, we played one another like a symphony, fine-tuning our bodies to touch, sipping wine, licking it from our hot, slick flesh. Satiated, we slept.

*****

My car was missing from the church lot the next morning. As it turned out, the unapologetic secretary, who also happened to be the preacher's wife, had it towed into downtown Crawfordville before she left to go home that night. The woman appeared to feel completely justified when she saw the crumpled condition we were in.

At the church office, she stared at us in distaste when I asked, "Excuse me, I work for the paper in Tallahassee and I'm looking for my car. It's a green Subaru. I left it here yesterday thinking it would be safe at a church."

"Yes, I saw it; you've left it here before, haven't you?" At my nod, she continued in a dispassionate voice. "I saw the press card in the

4

window, but our insurance won't allow cars to be left here overnight. I called Rosebud Towing. You know them? They're woman-owned. You can't miss the storefront. It's pink like their trucks."

We feared meeting anyone we knew, especially reporters from the Wakulla News, but nothing of the sort happened. Instead, the waywardness of it cemented our bond. Arriving at the Rosebud Towing impoundment lot to bail my car in broad daylight, our clothes were crumpled, I was in less than optimal condition, and Jason had a dark shadow on his chin.

We were greeted with amused expressions by the two women behind the counter. It was obvious they'd seen this scenario play out before and thought it funny. While it was clear the whole thing was *old hat* to them, it was incredibly embarrassing to me.

Just before I climbed into my car, one of the drivers cooed into my ear as only a woman can do, "If you're gonna' stay out overnight, sweetheart, you'd best keep a brush in your purse."

Gritting my teeth, I pulled out of the lot, leaving her laughing in my wake, determined never to let myself get caught like that again. That determination lasted about one day. I was at the paper in the storage room looking for something in the back issues shelves when Jason walked in, closed the door, turned out the light, and took me in his arms.

"Jason, don't you think we should be more careful?" I whispered. Before I could say anything more his lips stopped mine; my body's immediate response overcame any objections I might have had. It also put me in a completely untenable situation with my co-workers. From that day forward, I walked a delicate tightrope between trying to do my job, keeping my hormones under control, and retaining what little dignity I had left. A part of me didn't care what anybody thought.

Our affair rapidly ripened into a thing of exquisite torture; we simply couldn't stay away from one another no matter where we were. All I could think about were the powerful feelings he aroused.

Taking chances, seeing and touching him off and on at the office, the giddy combination of satiation from sex, and the wicked lure of dirty talk was intoxicating. Unfortunately, preoccupation with the man I worked for also served to settle me, dampening the ambitions I'd brought to the paper.

The situation at work was especially difficult during disagreements, and we had many. That's also what eventually restored me to sanity. Jason as editor-in-chief was my immediate boss, therefore, interaction with him was constant whether we feuded or not. Irritating too, were the sly looks other staff members gave us, not to mention the steely stare in the publisher's icy blue eyes.

Eventually, I noticed their focused attention to front-page article placement. This attention caused me no end of discomfort because I knew the other staff writers were on guard for favoritism, no matter that I was already the lead writer before Jason's arrival.

I couldn't blame them—I would have done the same, but I don't think Jason gave me preferential treatment. His loyalty to the paper was paramount, if a bit skewed, in order to make himself look good.

Wednesday, when we gathered in the editorial room to get the week's assignments, the publisher told us she wanted full-scale coverage on a new development just south of the Capitol. In spite of its proximity to the state's seat of power, this was a quadrant that failed to prosper with the rest of the city. I salivated at the prospect of digging into the reasons for the sudden interest in the area.

With our paper's slightly left-wing skew and willingness to tackle unpopular topics, one might have thought our publisher would dress in a more bohemian style, but such was not the case. Instead, she dressed in a conservative, highly professional manner. Today's ensemble, one of her many exquisite business suits, was baby blue with a mandarin collar topped off with pearls.

Completely comfortable in her own skin and very sure of herself, Melinda sat forward to address us. "Things are changing fast on the south side of town, and I want you all to stay on top of it. Now that the old Capital Ball Field is rebuilt as Cascades Park, I want to know what is happening, where the money is coming from, and what people in surrounding neighborhoods think about it. We'll make it a series, covering the development from the ground up. Let's see what happens."

Leaning back, she gave the floor to her editor-in-chief to distribute the week's assignments.

"Sheila, I need you to take the South Monroe Street flyover. Talk to people on the street, see how they view it. Find out if anybody uses the thing and how much it cost taxpayers to build it. Matt, go with her, take the pictures we need and then meet Mari at the Old Jail down by the Cascades park. Word has it a developer with big ideas wants to tear it down and build restaurants and high rises down there. Make sure you cover the story of that old oak tree on the corner that is bound to suffer. There are a lot of memories about it among the Tallahassee natives, so I want a big spread with lots of photographs—history, community sentiment—you name it. Show us the place. Jackson, you go down there with them and do a man-on-the-street piece about what's happening."

I saw the eyebrows raise when he gave me the Old Jail assignment, but it was perfect for me. I'd been concerned about the old live oak that stood sentinel near the building for some time. It was well over two-hundred-years-old, but I knew it was endangered by new development. My grandmother remembered seeing it when she went to the farmer's market with her father in the 1930s. At that time, it was huge with sprawling limbs and a wide circumference. Now it was mostly a knobby black trunk, most of the broad-reaching limbs were gone, and Gaines Street was too close, smothering the roots.

Working on this project, I grew tired of the intrigue surrounding my relationship with Jason. I hated the innuendo at the office and disliked my craven need for him.

When I finally made it clear that I didn't want to see him anymore, he flatly refused to believe it.

"Jason, I'm done. Our relationship is over," I told him over lunch one day. "It's doing nothing for me."

"How can you say that," he said. "Think about last night. Are you willing to give that up?"

He had a point. We were always a hot number in bed, but I wanted more. "Look, Jason, there should be a lot more to relationships than sex, but that's all ours is now. Besides that, I hate the looks the other staff give me. I no longer have a single friend on this paper."

7

"Yes, you do," he said, putting a finger to my lips. "You have me. That's all you need." For a time, I believed him.

He redoubled his efforts to keep me on his string. My desk's placement put my back to him at the office, giving him the advantage of surprise. He knew that I could sense his animal aura even when I couldn't see him. Knowing my involuntary response, he invented opportunities to touch, hover, or pass too close to me. Flowers and notes littered my desk, small gifts, invitations to dinner, tickets to concerts, and even a flashy brochure for a cruise to Bermuda. It's hard to admit, even now, that his gifts impaired my judgment, but for a time they and his closeness exerted pressure I couldn't resist.

I am ashamed to say that I let him bring some of his stuff back to my place. For a brief while, we again inhabited that strange ecstasy-fueled existence we'd known before, but it didn't last. Sex, no matter how titillating, grows old when there's little to no substance beyond it.

Gradually, I found his small imperfections profoundly irritating. His crooked, lower front teeth caught my attention. I thought that stupid-looking curl drooping on his forehead juvenile. His scent on the sheets made me nauseated, and I hated his toothpaste spatters on the bathroom mirror.

I grew to hate finding Jason's personal detritus littering the floor throughout my apartment; I wanted the man out of my life but I didn't have the guts to make it happen. Spineless on my own, it took an encounter with a white dog to permanently sever our connection.

Driving back from an interview in Gadsden County late one afternoon, a blur of white collided with the car just ahead of mine. Bits of pale fur and flesh flew into the late afternoon's golden light, splashing my windshield with dark, red blood. Figuring it was a dog, and without thinking twice about the wisdom of what I was about to do, I pulled off the highway to see what I could do to help.

The man who'd hit him stopped to drag the animal out of traffic. By the time I pulled over, the big white dog lay crumpled against the guardrail, covered in blood with exposed muscle and gristle. While the driver inspected the damage to his pickup, I checked the dog to see if anything could be done to relieve its suffering.

The whole left side was mangled and leaking body fluids onto the asphalt. Bits of bone that should have been connected protruded at odd angles, but the lungs continued to draw air. Why was this dog among the living? It just didn't seem possible.

"Leave it, woman. The damned fool dog is barely alive." He was walking away when I heard him mutter, "How in tarnation it got over the fence is beyond me."

I looked down at the dog that should have died but was still holding onto life. For one brief moment, he looked at me, his blue eyes filled with pain. In the midst of incredible distress, the soul of that animal touched mine. After that, there was no turning back.

"This dog is suffering," I replied, yelling over the noisy traffic, "We cannot leave him here like this. At least help me get it into my car."

Head down, his still-bloody hands held carefully away from his body, the man reluctantly retraced his steps. By that time, the dog was groaning and trying to move.

"I've got a friend near here, a veterinarian. He'll save this animal if anybody can. Please help me!"

When the man shook his head slightly, I knew he wanted nothing more to do with either me or the dog. I, however, couldn't abandon the animal. In response to his resistance, I grew even more determined.

Attempting to lift the big dog by myself, I found that I could not. This, at least, provoked the driver to action. Relenting in the face of my doggedness, the nameless man fetched a spattered paint cloth out of his car, cursing under his breath, and brought it to me. In silence, we turned it into a makeshift body sling.

Struggling with the dog's dead-weight, we got him into the back of my hatchback where it began to heave. Heedless of the blood and the puke, I dabbed at the spew, hastily threw my jacket over him, and then turned to the driver.

Before I could say anything, he stopped me saying, "I couldn't avoid hitting that poor dog, you know. I'm glad it's still alive and all, but I can't help pay for it. Better to have let it die."

I failed to consider the matter of payment for that moment, but I was committed to the mission by then. I had to get help for that blue-eyed dog. Shaking my head in response, I slid into my car and reached for the phone.

Obviously relieved, the man drove away while I called Tim at the Emergency Animal Hospital with a plea for help.

"Hey, Tim, it's me, Marianna Ross. I found an injured dog on the side of I-10. Can I bring him to your clinic?"

"Sure," he said, having helped me with other rescues in the past. "bring 'em in. We're slow at the moment."

His staff was waiting for us at the back entrance when I pulled in. Surprisingly, after losing copious amounts of blood and then hurling its guts out, the dog was still alive but just barely. Judging from their expressions, I knew it was probably hopeless, but they were determined to try.

Tim was not, however, prepared for the extent of the white dog's injuries, which were extensive. "Good Lord, Mari! Look at this poor dog!" he said when staff pulled him from the rear of the car. "How on earth is it still alive?"

All business now, he ushered me out of the room, then began preparations for surgery.

To keep myself occupied while Tim and his team worked, I cleaned the car as best I could, throwing the spread and ruined jacket into the dumpster. Thinking I'd have the car detailed the next day I settled myself in the waiting room to make phone calls. That's when it occurred to me that I'd completely forgotten my boyfriend and the special dinner he'd planned.

After telling him what transpired and where I was, I got a barrage of accusations about why I hadn't called earlier. "Did you just conveniently forget our dinner reservations at Georgio's at eight p.m.?" he asked. "I called them at nine when I couldn't get you to answer the phone. They were not pleased."

It was typical of him to attack first, but I was unprepared for what he aimed at me next. "What the fuck are you doing rescuing an injured stray off the highway?"

I wondered why on earth I bothered to call him at all, but in the interest of peace I tried to placate him, saying, "I saw it happen, Jason! I couldn't just drive away and leave that dog to die."

My explanation fell on deaf ears, and Jason hung up on me.

Stewing in my own juice, my spirits plummeted. I spent the next several hours reading ancient magazines and pulling up books on my iPhone but couldn't concentrate. After what seemed like hours, Tim came out to tell me that the dog would survive, that it was a German Shepherd mix, and that there was an odd tattoo on the right shoulder.

"It's not real clear," he said of the mark, "but it looks like the Chi Rho from ancient Greece or maybe early Christianity to me. Never saw it on an animal before. Could be part of an elite pack of guard dogs. I tried to pull it up, but nothing like that came up on the registries. There's no chip."

I later discovered the symbol in pre-Christian antiquity signified Good Fortune.

Bandaged and splinted, it seemed only the dog's head escaped damage. What I didn't know at the time was the action of saving him set off a chain of events that changed my own life.

Personally committed to the dog by that time, I told Tim I'd cover the bill if he was willing to break it into payments, which, thankfully, he was. Then I climbed into my smelly car and drove home in North Florida's dense pre-dawn fog.

It was pushing 4 a.m. when I reached the apartment. The lights were on and Jason was waiting up for me. He met me at the door, bleary-eyed in his boxer shorts and the night's stubble on his face, both barrels loaded.

Without preamble, and sounding just like my dearly departed father, he yelled, "Marianna, what have you got yourself into this time!" It was as though I were an irresponsible child who did this kind of thing all the time. Then came, "How could you be so selfish?"

Already shocked by everything I had seen and heard, and much too tired to think clearly, I tried to explain.

"Jason, I'm sorry for not calling you but this was one of the most horrific things I've ever seen—"

He interrupted before I could finish. "You were supposed to be home by 6:30. We had reservations at Georgios's and everything. Did you call to let me know you'd be late so that I could cancel? No. Did you answer my calls? NO. When you finally checked in at midnight, it was to say you'd rescued a dog stupid enough to try and cross a busy highway. I just don't believe it!"

He had a point, several actually, but it was what came next that tangled my nerves beyond endurance. "That was a crazy, insane thing to do, picking up a mangled mutt off of the highway. Then you took it to the emergency vet's office after hours. Dogs do crazy things when they are in pain. It could have bitten you. My God, did the potential for rabies occur to you?"

Following closely on the heels of this statement came the bombshell that eventually blew us apart. "Who's going to pay the bill, Mari? It won't be me, and I don't think you should spend your hard-earned money like that. Get your precious Tim to put it down. I'll pay for that."

Stunned by Jason's verbal assault, which hit me square in the middle of my already fragile gut, I staggered mentally. I had not asked for his help with the dog, financial or otherwise, but there he was, berating me about it as though I was a recalcitrant child.

I stalked into my bedroom and slammed the door, locking him out of it and my heart. His words angered me deeply, stirring something that had been simmering in the back of my mind for a long time. He's selfish and domineering. I don't need him or his arrogance.

The next morning Jason was up and gone with the sun. Relieved that I wouldn't have to deal with him first thing, I dressed and left for an early interview and then followed several leads, avoiding the office.

Mid-afternoon, I went in to write the story, ignoring the almighty Jason Petersen as though he never existed. That got the staff's attention. Eyebrows arched and looks darted around cubicles because they were accustomed to our quick visits to the storeroom on my arrival, not my walking to the other side of the room to avoid him. Jason left soon after without speaking to me.

Knowing looks fitted over and around the desks, but I said nothing to illuminate them. Jason and I had grossly neglected discretion; I saw that now, but it was far too late to try and fix the error. Let them think what they would—our affair was none of their business.

It still amazes me that I was able to focus, but the article about a Korean War veteran came together easily. I finished it on deadline, tidied up my desk, and went home to an empty apartment.

At first, it was a relief to have the place to myself, but then I began to miss the man who'd absorbed my very being for the past two years. Our breakup was too fast, leaving loose ends dangling that had yet to fray.

Jason and I made up in a week or so, but things were different between us from that time on. Some part of me knew that I needed to reclaim myself, but it took a crippled dog to make it happen.

Looking back, I can see where fate was leading, but at the time I was blind to it.

*****

After two months the white dog not only survived, but he made a vigorous recovery. His extended stay also racked up an enormous bill for which I was responsible. The dog's response to me helped to push that unfortunate fact into a figment of the distant future.

"Look at you, sweet doggie," I cooed to him the first time I went in. "Aren't you getting to be a beauty." To which the as yet un-named dog wagged his tail and tried to stand on his bandaged and splinted legs. "Oh, no, not yet. Stay there. I'll come to you."

As though the white Shepherd understood my words, he settled back into his blankets and flicked his big pointed ears, waiting. Thus began a getting-to-know-you period, during which I completely lost my heart. But I wasn't the only one who fell for him.

One of his new buddies, Angie, the black three-legged office cat, moved into his kennel to keep him company 24/7. In that loving atmosphere, the big Shepherd with the knowing spirit became a favorite, and everyone dreaded the day of his departure.

"Tim, do you think he's well enough that I could take him home and foster him from there?" I asked. "I know he's got a long way to go, but the bill is rising faster than my income. Once he's well, then you can put him up for adoption. What do you think?"

"I know it's rough on you, but I don't think he's well enough to leave here just yet. Besides, you can take as long as you need for the bill," he told me. "If it was only me, I wouldn't have charged you anything, but his surgery was extensive, and the recovery intensive on the part of my staff."

I knew that already, but the continued visits and rising medical costs were becoming a challenge. Besides, Jason, who resented my visits and every penny I spent, kept pointing out that Tim and I needed to find the dog's owner and get "it" off our hands.

Finally, with only the odd Chi Rho tattoo on his shoulder, no collar, no chip, and no legitimate response to our ads in the classifieds, Tim called to tell me the Shepherd was ready for adoption. Something like panic gripped my heart when I heard those words, but I pushed it down hard. There was no way that I could adopt him at that point. I already owed too much from trying to get him patched up and able to walk.

"Okay," I responded with dread. "Let's post it on Facebook to see what happens."

Knowing an animal like him was highly desirable even healing from his injuries, and that he would leave quickly, I went by to see him at lunch. Tim's Facebook page was already filling up with offers from all over the country, so I knew it might be the last time I'd see the big white dog I had come to love.

When I got there, he was calmly sitting in the kennel grooming little Angie who was asleep nestled between his front paws. Instead of leaping up in recognition or barking when he saw me like he usually did, those staggering blue eyes simply looked into mine with calm recognition. Then he cocked his head and flicked those big ears in greeting so as not to disturb the sleeping cat.

That's when the idea of his going to someone else struck me as wrong; the thought was completely untenable.

"I cannot let him go," I heard myself say.

Tim grinned and nodded his head at the staff who'd gathered around. "That's our girl. We knew that dog was going to be yours the minute you brought it in. Nobody takes that kind of care for an animal without falling for it. As far as I'm concerned, it was meant to be."

Moving quickly, and without giving Jason a second thought, I adopted the dog that same day. Borrowing a leash from Tim, we took leave of the office staff and Angie and set out for home. While it was very awkward for him to walk and apparently quite painful, my beautiful new dog tried to clown around all the way to the car.

Laughing, I carefully loaded him into the back seat, telling him to stay. He remained there all of five minutes before gingerly making his way to the front. This was not an easy task in my small hatchback that had very little room between the front seats. Undeterred, he squeezed through in what was surely a painful maneuver, turned around a couple of times, his tail fanning my face in the process, and settled down. Securing the passenger side for his own he turned to me with a big grin on his face and then looked out the window like a fully sentient being.

What could I say? My heart singing in response to my new companion's antics, I named him Rambo. Considering what happened next, the name choice was appropriate.

Rattling around in the back of my mind was the vague thought that once Jason met the dog his resistance would melt and things would go back to what passed for normal with us. Not so. The minute that skinny dog limped over the threshold of my apartment, mutual antipathy sprang to life between them.

Their hatred for one another was immediate, total, and unforgiving. Jason sprang to his feet, yelling at me for bringing Rambo home. Sensing an enemy in the room, Rambo locked eyes with Jason and, ignoring his injuries, growled. He then headed straight for the man; his wolf-like fangs barred.

Had not the dog been so fierce and the man so frightened, it might have been amusing.

Affronted, Jason backed up, cursing at first. Then realizing the dog owned the territory, he let his pretension go and tried to hide behind the sofa. Wrong move. My dog began to stalk towards him, determination in each step. Frightened by what was happening, I yelled at Rambo, telling him to halt. For some reason, he responded, but it was with obvious reluctance that he did it.

The insult in what he considered his second home was too much for the man to handle. Keeping his back to the wall, Jason worked his way to the door, grabbed his car keys from the hall table and fled, spelling the absolute end of our relationship.

Once my heart stopped pounding, the whole thing got funny. To my way of thinking, the dog's actions were impressive. Certainly, they were far more effective than my puny efforts to expunge Jason from my life. Laughing, I sank onto the sofa while Rambo took possession of his new surroundings, pacing through them until he was satisfied his dastardly foe was gone. Watching him survey the rooms, the notion that he was a security canine in his past life was confirmed in my mind. It was obvious that he had extensive training and knew what to do in a compromising situation. That he was firmly bonded to me was a relief.

That night I couldn't get away from Jason's scent on the sheets, but I was too tired to do anything about it. Instead, comforted by my nice, furry friend on the floor next to me, I fell asleep almost immediately.

Morning found Rambo curled up in Jason's former spot with my ex-boyfriend's offending pillow ripped to shreds on the floor. I simply could not find it in my heart to be angry, and I secretly applauded his actions. Reaching for Rambo—who, I was learning, tolerated affection when necessary—I hugged him close, nuzzling his snowy, white ears.

He tolerated the affection as long as needed, but once he thought I was done, it was over. Dropping awkwardly off the bed, Rambo headed towards the kitchen and then stopped halfway to see if I was coming, the expression in his blue eyes so human it was startling.

With a laugh, I followed him to the kitchen, fed him, and then let my new companion out into the fenced backyard. Amazed by his recovery and boundless energy, I watched him try to romp and play with his new toys in awe. Though extremely awkward with his left side and bandaged legs, Rambo was a living, breathing miracle.

On our return to the kitchen, I took out a raw bone purchased just for him and watched him toss it in the air before wrangling with it on the braided rug. Knowing we had just set a precedent, I told him, "You big brute of a dog, all you wanted was to bribe me so you could get a treat!"

Ignoring me, my dog gnawed away with a sideways grin on his silly face while I stared in dismay at the white hair already coating the rug.

As it was Rambo's first day in my home and I had no safe place for him to stay while I was at work, I called in sick. My first priority was to procure a kennel and a good harness for him, so we took our first trip to the pet store together. There, he managed to charm everyone in no time flat.

"So this is the dog you found on I-10," said one of the clerks, admiring him. She helped me fit him with a good harness that I could manage and would be comfortable for him, and then said, "We all loved the stories you wrote about him in the paper and hoped you would adopt him."

It was flattering to know folks actually read what I wrote and knew who I was. I basked in the notoriety for a moment, but the feeling was fleeting; Rambo and I had business to attend to back at the apartment. It was time for the big cleanse.

The apartment was a disaster area: I had a new dog and all of his gear to find places for, and I had just dumped a messy boyfriend. The first priority when we got home was to remove Jason's belongings. The man was known to drop his personal effects any which way, but Rambo went after them with a purposeful vengeance. Once found, he shredded some of the more private items. Surprised by the amount of Jason's stuff that littered my home, I tossed lone socks found in the strangest places— some already given the Rambo treatment—toothbrushes, and razors. Books and clothes went into a plastic bag. Finding a disgusting pair of silk orange and blue University of Florida Gator boxer shorts under the bed, I gave them to my dog with the promise to be more careful with whom I shared myself in the future.

17

The refrigerator held Jason's favorite beer, and a carton of unopened premium chocolate mint ice cream that I would never eat lurked in the freezer. I threw most of the perishables away but gave my neighbors the unopened food and the ice cream. I resolved to finish packing the rest of his stuff to take into work the next day.

All this done, I drank a diet cola laced with Captain Morgan rum and then proceeded to study the apartment with disfavor. While the stemmed greenware glasses, my comfy leather chair and its ottoman, the colorful, timeworn Mexican chairs, and a Thai rubbing held a certain rustic appeal, little beyond them did. It was clearly time for a change.

By the time I crawled into my fresh, sun-dried sheets for the night, I was resolved to find new work and leave my job, let the apartment go, keep my favorite pieces, and sell or give away the rest. As it turns out, the universe conspired to help me keep that promise to myself sooner than anticipated.

Chapter 2

Things pretty much settled into a routine between Rambo and me after cleaning Jason's detritus out of our lives. Enrolling him in obedience school, I soon discovered he was pretty well trained already. What he needed was direction from me, so I became the student. I soon figured out the signals he recognized, and we both learned new ones. As his healing continued, we took long walks in Tallahassee's moss-draped parks, met other dogs with their owners, tossed balls, played hide & seek, and learned to trust one another.

Rambo had been with me for several weeks when I came in from work one afternoon and discovered a response to my application from the Roan Mountain Writers Residency Program in the mail. Almost afraid of what I might find, but far too eager to wait, I tore into it.

The Roan Mountain, Tennessee Writers Residency Program

March 18, 2016
Dear Ms. Ross,
On behalf of the Roan Mountain Writers Residency selection committee, I would like to congratulate you on your successful application to our program. If you choose to accept this invitation, your tenure is expected to begin August 31 and run through November 30, 2016.

You will reside in the furnished Residency cabin during your stay with an additional stipend direct-deposited the first of each month into your personal bank account.

We believe the Appalachian people native to Roan Mountain are unique to American culture. As such, their stories tell the tale; it is their ancestral stories that we wish to secure for future generations. Your credentials as a reporter and training in oral history collection make you ideal for this opportunity. We look forward to working with you and will provide any assistance you may require in the effort to collect and preserve the history of our mountain community.

Please sign and return the attached contract at your earliest convenience. Additional information to assist you in making plans for time with us is available online at our website, www.storymountain.org.

Sincerely,

Christopher Papadis

It was the confirmation of what I wanted most in life—the coveted residency that would take me to the mountains of Upper East Tennessee; all I, Marianna Ross, had to do was accept.

That's as far as I got. The minute I turned the doorknob, Rambo pressed his long thin nose against the door until he was able to wriggle through. He then proceeded to dance around me bandages or no. Trying hard to frown and scold, I lost the battle to laughter as we engaged in our daily homecoming ritual.

My welcome assured, Rambo headed to the back door for his coveted time outside while I focused on the award letter. My mission would be to collect the oral histories of residents native to Roan Mountain. In addition, I would present interactive workshops at the Cloudland community center nearby. The result would be a book published under my name listed as "editor."

I could see the cover already, *Life Stories: The People of Roan Mountain*, edited by Marianna Ross. Sweet. Long delayed and nearly abandoned, visions of adventure and success suddenly awakened to shimmer on the horizon.

Letter in hand, I plopped down on the sofa to look for loopholes. There weren't any. It was clear, succinct, and almost daunting.

I shared the news first with Cassie, my life-long friend. I frequently ran ideas past her before taking them further. She had a way of clarifying things and often gave the kind of advice only a best friend can do, but when I called her, instead of support, I got a nasty surprise.

"Cassie, you'll never believe what came in the mail today. It's a letter of acceptance from the Roan Mountain Writer's Residency. I got it!"

Perplexed by her lack of response, I hollered into the phone, "Don't you remember?—the writing residency—the one on Roan Mountain in Tennessee.... You proofed the proposal!"

Still nothing from the other end of the line. "Cassie, I'm going to Tennessee. I'm gonna' live and write in the wilderness for three whole months!"

When she finally responded, secure in her role as my advisor, Cassie accidentally provided the final nudge I needed to leap off the cliff and grasp the future with both hands.

"Well, good for you, Mari," she said in a sardonic voice filled with reservation. "I know the competition was stiff. I'm sure it's a great honor to receive an award such as this, but there are some things you need to consider before accepting it."

Then without warning, it was as though a switch flipped; she was off and running, leaving me breathless in her wake. "I know it's only for three months, but you'll need to think hard and long before accepting that award. You'll be giving up your life to go 600 miles away just so you can write stories. That's something you can do right here. Be realistic Mari, you need a regular salary, people, and creature comforts, not a rustic cabin in the boonies. Think about it. You'll probably be alone most of the time. Is that really what you want?"

That was my friend Cassie for you—the yen to my yang. She had a talent for putting her finger on my tender points and pushing down hard. I usually tolerated her ministrations because they were on target, but this time she executed a hatchet job I couldn't accept, slicing me into ribbons with a finely sharpened blade.

Surprised by what I heard in her voice, I wanted to figuratively slap her upside the head. Instead, she jumped back into the fray before I could say anything.

"Marianna, you're starry-eyed over this thing. I'm sorry to throw cold water on you, but listen to me—it's great they've offered you this opportunity but you're a fool to even consider it. You've got your career at the paper well in hand. It's not glamorous, but it's steady, and you've got insurance and a measure of security. And then there's Jason. I know it's an on and off again thing, but there is potential for a long-lasting relationship with him if you work at it. Besides, you must admit you are no longer a bright-eyed twenty-something."

Speechless and above all dismayed, I sank back into my chair to consider her comments. She scored a minor point about the job, but the barb about my age, that one I rejected outright. In my mid-twenties, I was far from ready to settle down to the hubby, cottage, and babies. Besides, the fling with Jason was over, she just didn't know it yet.

Accustomed as she was to my admiring attention, Cassie plowed ahead, unaware she was preaching to an unresponsive audience. From the back of my mind came the thought: I desperately need change, and she knows it, so why is she suddenly playing the devil's advocate?

It was then a revelation struck me: her wings, practically cemented shut, held her earthbound, while mine were unfurling like those of a baby dragon ready for first flight.

"Anyway," she continued, trampling my reverie with lead feet, "you'd better think long and hard about where you'll be after the three months is up. Oh, and there's another thing…" I wanted to hang up on her. "…I looked it up, and that cabin you'll live in all by yourself," this said with solemn emphasis, "hangs off the side of that mountain. It's surrounded by a bunch of giant trees, and you'll probably be alone the whole time except for occasional hikers—people you don't know, Mari—think about strangers knocking on your door in the wilderness. Your only company will be hawks, bears, and mountain lions, or

22

whatever they call wild cats up there. And then there's snow and blizzards to think about."

That's when I knew the universe had at long last heard my plea for change. I wanted everything she described, and I wanted it bad enough to leave my present life behind. The notion of the flight was not only tantalizing; it was within my grasp, and I was ready to embrace it. And I would not be alone, that I knew for certain. Rambo would go with me.

As though agreeing with my decision, Rambo growled directly at the phone. A quick pat on the head settled him down but failed to satisfy me. Perhaps my job and boyfriend weren't the only things I should leave behind. Who was Cassie to berate me like that?

Realistically, though I tried to ignore her dire warnings, I had to admit that some of what my dark prophet said might be true except the part about the weather—the contract was for late summer and fall—not winter. I would be up there when the leaves turned, not for wintertime's heavy snow and ice. When we hung up, I didn't care if I ever spoke to Cassie again. Cracks and crevasses that formed over the years between us split into an impassable gulf.

Setting her scathing commentary aside, I turned to the task of completing acceptance of the award. Fairly certain of a positive response in a different sector, I called my mother.

Enthusiastic when she heard the news, Mom encouraged me to embrace change and to make the leap into the unknown. Our conversation, which was completely affirming, made me wonder why I put off telling her for last. But then there were some good reasons for my reluctance: my mom isn't your average matron. She can be capricious and unpredictable but this time she was supportive. When I told her about Cassie's pontification, Mom morphed into the Good Fairy. I had a hunger for flight and she fed the fire.

"I'm so proud of you, darling," she cooed into the phone. "It's about time someone recognized your talent. Don't worry about what Cassie said; that girl's jealous of you. That's her problem, not yours. When do you leave?"

Let me describe my mom before going on. A financially independent widow, sensual and still quite lovely in her late forties, she's

23

a hopeless male magnet. She delights in attracting a wide assortment of unsuspecting men into her lair, including some of my boyfriends. Needless to say, her bohemian ways have caused some problems between us, but when I need her, she's there for me.

"Do it, Mari. Do it now while you can. Leave here, and don't let anything stop you, especially not that dead-end job at the newspaper. It has taken you nowhere fast and you know it. If they refuse to give you a leave of absence, so be it. Forget what Cassie said—she's stuck and she knows it. As for Jason, let him go, too. You need to find someone more suited to your independent nature. Leave it all behind and shake the dust of this place from your feet."

Like a dragon with its hatchling, my mother encouraged me to test my wings, neither knowing nor caring about the tempests and gales that she knew would come my way. The flight was everything.

And so it was that I made the momentous decision to leave both the paper and the man in my wake. I had some doubts, however, about leaving my mom to her own devices. Some of her escapades could easily fill the pages of a hot, steamy romance novel. Knowing it was useless to try to control her, I concluded that her affairs were none of my business as long as she stayed out of mine.

Chapter 3

Two days later, still peeved by her tirade but unwilling to lose her friendship, I called Cassie. We met for Asian at one of those artsy little cafés Tallahassee has in abundance, this one nestled in the basement of a repurposed church. Now sullied by its lust for filthy lucre, the dark and almost subversive intimacy of the place appealed to me that night. Converted to eclectic shops and music rooms, it housed an Asian restaurant and a tattoo parlor in the basement catacombs. The sanctuary above hosted a recording studio whose eclectic music reverberated throughout the building.

Protective armor strapped in place, lightsaber at the ready to protect myself, I entered that strange, dark place with its pulsating vibes. As was her custom, Cassie was already there so she could snag a table to her liking. As a result, my back was usually to the window.

At first glance on entering, I recoiled. What I saw was scary. Somehow, Cassie's mop of curly red hair was backlit against the deep red of those painted concrete blocks. It looked like she was on fire.

The horror must have shown on my face because she broke the spell with a laugh, saying, "Is something wrong? You look like you've seen a ghost or something."

Truth to tell, I had seen a ghostly aura around her. Brushing that thought aside, I copped a lie. "No, sorry. It's just so dark in here. It took a minute for my eyes to adjust."

Joining her, my eyes quickly adapted to the bizarre atmosphere. I could see it was just Cassie, my old friend and not some ogre, but the unease with her remained.

We ordered, played with our chopsticks, and then danced around the real reason we were there. I was intent on leaving Tallahassee, and she was just as determined to keep me bogged down in my native environs.

No sooner did our drinks arrive than she struck the first snide blow. "So, are you still going to be a famous Appalachian writer?"

Affronted, I sat back in my chair and stared at her. Dammit, what I really wanted from my best friend was someone who would talk sanely with me, not berate and cut down everything I wanted to accomplish.

In the face of Cassie's cynicism, I deflected the slam with one of my own. "Yes. I sent the contract yesterday. It's better than staying here and never trying to climb the mountain at all."

I will admit the reality of what I was about to do had begun to penetrate the dream. An ugly specter, let's call it fear, emerged from the depths of my consciousness. Now it had a face—milky white topped by fiery red hair.

Suddenly, the exaggerated punk rock beat from above filtered through block walls painted the color of blood. It poured through that defiled sanctuary to consume me with sudden anger.

So sure was Cassie of her rightness that my interrogator failed to realize she was hanging herself on a cross and that I had a figurative spear at the ready.

"You're really going to quit your job aren't you," she continued, taking a sip of blood red wine. "I can't believe you'd do something so foolhardy. I mean, are you crazy? You'll be living in God-forsaken mountain country. What if something happens to you and you get hurt, raped in the backwoods, or God forbid, some crazy person tries to kill you, and think about this: will your smartphone function up there?"

Shades of crimson wavered before my face when I interrupted her. "I'm going to Roan Mountain, and there's nothing you can do to stop me. Why are you trying to hold me back?"

Those words set her off on a rant that made me feel the sparks flying from her mouth. The restaurant was filling by that time and heads turned her direction. By the time Cassie finally ran down, the coveted Ming Chicken lay congealed on my plate, the rice had dried into little white pellets, delectable pork dumplings lay on their sides in the last throes, and the Pinot Noir sat sour on my stomach.

Without another word to her smug self, I got a to-go box, asked for my check, gathered my things, and left. Almost home my stomach rebelled, and it took all I could do to make it to the house without a disaster.

An astute observer of his personal human, Rambo could sense trouble miles away from the very beginning of our friendship. He met me at the door with unusual calm instead of his usual excitement. A ghostly shadow, he padded behind me to the bathroom, waited patiently as I emptied the contents of my stomach, and then walked me to the bedroom, tail wagging slowly, big ears on alert.

Collapsing on the bed, I let the tears pour while my dog gently curled up next to me, one big paw planted squarely in the pit of my back, still on alert.

It should not be so complex for a grown woman to leave home, I thought. After a while, a cold nose touched my arm, Rambo's way of making sure I was going to be all right. Wrapping my arms around his big furry self I took comfort from his benign presence.

*****

My mother, when I told her about the debacle with Cassie, laughed in that merry way she has, and congratulated me on leaving the woman in my wake. She even offered to let me store some things in the garage and in my old bedroom. Clearly, Cassie's strange behavior was beneath her notice.

"I can definitely see that it is time for you to fly away for a while. I will keep your treasures while you're gone, and that will save storage costs. Consider it my contribution."

In the next breath, she changed the subject, catching me off-guard. "By the way, dear, Jason called the other day to tell me you two split up." A sharp little barb hit right where it would hurt the most. "I wasn't

27

at all surprised by the breakup, but I did wonder how long it would take for you to get around to telling me."

There wasn't much I could say. I waited a week to tell her…

*****

Without delay, I made an appointment to meet with the publisher immediately after the weekly staff meeting to discuss the residency.

Our publisher frequently absented herself from our editorial sessions so Jason ran it with his usual cool efficiency. Frankly, I was surprised by the paucity of assignments I got that day—just one—to get the story of a woman who made strawberry fudge in her microwave. Big deal.

I was still on the Cascades Park/Old Jail series, but this assignment felt like an affront. I take that back—it was a huge slap in the face. Had someone already told Jason and Melinda about my plans? Only my mom and Cassie knew up to that point…

Jason refused eye contact with me. Instead, he spoke to the staff photographer, "Matt, the governor is making an announcement about public health, so go with Jack to the Capitol today. Jeannie, there's a new rumor floating about developing the Chain of Parks downtown. Meet up with Matt when he leaves the Capitol. Snoop around, digging all the way down to the root of it." Then he turned to Matt, adding, "I want lots of pictures, especially those old oak trees. That's it, folks. Let's get to work."

What about me? I left the meeting red-faced and embarrassed by the cavalier treatment I received. Walking into Melinda's office filled with anger and apprehension was not the way I envisioned speaking with her.

Petite and perfectly coiffed, Melinda Burgher sat perched on her enormous office chair behind the huge wooden desk like an exquisite fairy queen.

"Come in, Marianna," she said, her voice almost dripping with sugary southern sweetness. Distant and cold, she projected a ridiculously powerful image for someone whose stature was so small.

There was something virulent in the room and it was much bigger than the little female dressed in the black designer skirt suit and pearls.

With infinite skill, she wielded her sword saying, "The office grapevine tells me you finally ended it with my editor-in-chief. Is this correct?"

My stomach was already tied up in knots, and caught off-guard, I chose to ignore the blunt question. Instead, I parried with a direct statement of my own.

"Melinda, I've accepted a three-month writing residency in East Tennessee. I would like to request a three-month leave-of-absence from the paper. The term begins—"

She cut me off, saying in a cold voice, "Oh, I've already heard about it, Marianna. It's old news; I was just waiting for you to get around to telling me. I'm sorry to tell you that if you leave now, your job here will end. I simply cannot hold it open for your eventual return. We need all of our writers on staff, not off chasing dreams."

While I was stunned by the coldness of her response, I was prepared for the next step. I took it quickly without giving myself a chance to back out. A soothing calmness took over, and I was able to move forward in control of myself without loss of dignity.

"It's good to know how little you value my work, Melinda but it's obvious to me that others do." Quickly, I pulled the letter from my jacket pocket and handed it out to her. "This is my formal letter of resignation. My four years with this paper were a great learning experience, but it's time to move on."

Taking the crisp white envelope in her perfectly manicured hand Melinda put it on her desk without bothering to open it. For some reason, my last thrust had taken her by surprise. If she expected me to grovel and beg for my job, she was disappointed. For the moment, she had nothing with which to parry, and while her aura still radiated danger, its focus had dissipated.

Glittering like daggers, her big china-blue eyes flicked towards the clear plate glass window separating the foyer from her private domain. Following that look, I sensed that someone had listened to our conversation, and that it was probably Jason. With that knowledge, something awakened, something that I had refused to acknowledge until that moment. Call it a fleeting whiff of intuition, a palpable impression possessed of an undercurrent of intrigue—whatever you wish to name it.

That thing pulsed to life briefly and disappeared, but not before I saw the truth.

The publisher and her editor-in-chief were involved, and she wanted me out of the way.

I finally accepted what I had tried to ignore: she was jealous! Insulated by the giddy delirium of what I thought of as love, I had taken Jason into my arms without ever thinking of who had come before or what it could do to me now.

To say the next two weeks were uncomfortable would be an understatement. Melinda stayed away from the office for a good portion of it, presumably taking vacation time. Jason kept to himself, eyes glued to his computer screen; the other staff writers followed his example, ignoring me completely. Even Matt, the photographer with whom I worked on several prize-winning projects and considered a good friend, avoided me. When he left on an assignment without a word, I began to feel adrift, so I called Marge the Fudge Lady and invited her to the office at noon for a demonstration.

Covering the editorial table with the makings for fudge including crushed strawberries and rich chocolate, I photographed the session myself. The work covered every available surface so that by the time Marge left, the scent of chocolate permeated every nook and cranny of that office and my statement was made. By way of a final statement, I took the strawberry fudge home with me after emptying my desk, leaving the mess behind for the staff to scrape and clean. For the next two weeks, I worked from there and nobody questioned me. Thus it was that without Jason and office innuendo to distract me, I worked prolifically and produced some of the best work of my newspaper career. My byline showed up long after I was no longer associated with that paper, and one of those stories earned an award. The strawberry fudge piece later won recognition from the food network.

Armed with this kind of irrefutable success I went to the exit interview, feeling sure of myself. Abandoning requisite business attire, I dressed in a crisp white shirt, gold hoop earrings, my favorite tweed jacket, and jeans finished off with a pair of hand-tooled boots.

The petite Melinda, this time dressed to the nines in an expensive navy-blue suit, matching three-inch pumps, and the ubiquitous pearls met me with a frosty smile. Something about her that day reminded me of a fairytale.

When I saw Melinda through those lenses, a good story came to mind, and it's the way I've thought of my former employer ever since. Ensconced in her executive power chair, she reminded me of little Miss Moppet sitting on a tuffet, eating her curds & whey, but I was the spider who sat down beside her.

Our conversation was stilted at first. Melinda could no longer dominate or fire me, so for a brief time, I felt powerful, too. I was leaving by my own choice, but I could tell from her body language that she still wanted to hurt me. I beat her to the draw by telling her I'd had enough of climbing the ladder to nowhere. In return, she glared at me with antipathy and then shook her perfect bouffant blonde head in disbelief.

"I gave you a chance to achieve something solid at this paper but I must tell you that you have not fulfilled my expectations." Seeing the quick anger in my eyes she altered course somewhat saying, "Mind you, your work has been acceptable, but that's all. Had it not been for Jason Petersen, I would have let you go long ago."

That hurt; my armor wasn't tough enough to withstand the lance she cruelly shot through it, but deep down I no longer cared. I rose to leave but not before I told her exactly what I felt about the past four years spent at her paper.

"And who said this was a good newspaper, Melinda?" Her face paled visibly at this, so I continued. "Four years I performed the grunt reporter's ritual, interviewing politicians and executives and their grandiose plans for our town. I tracked down rumors and scandals and listened to recently transplanted retirees gush on about our fair community and their dreams for changing it. I visited art-filled kitchens to check out fabulous chefs and their dishes but never got a bite. I wrote about special events, birthdays for antiquarians, and anything to do with small children and animals. In addition, I worked to help save the canopy roads from development, won several awards, and took great pride in my accomplishments, and you have the nerve to sit there and tell me my work was just, 'acceptable.'"

Melinda's left eye was twitching uncontrollably when I walked out of her glass office. One of her tiny shoes lay on its side next to her executive chair, but I didn't see it. I never looked back.

Getting into my car, my father's last words came to me. Uttered on his deathbed, they tolled dark and loud. "Just promise me you'll finish college and get a nice, stable job teaching at a university or with the state. Find a good man who loves you and who will take care of you. Marry him, Marianna; have his children, and be safe and happy."

Being an honest sort of person, I evaded responding to his request even though it was his last, because I already knew nice, safe jobs and good men bored me half to death. He died without seeing his hatchling settled into a nicely feathered nest of her own, never knowing that she would fly clean out of the coup.

Now, I had cut the cords to both my profession and what I had once considered a promising relationship to fly unfettered into uncharted waters with no intention of return. Dad's words fluttered like dry leaves falling to the ground.

Chapter 4

With time on my hands and nothing to do but make plans, I called the grant administrator to ask about possibly renting the cabin for a couple of weeks before my formal contract began. That's also when it occurred to me that I failed to make mention of my dog when we made the arrangements. Of course, I didn't know Rambo when I made the application, but he was a big part of my life now, and I couldn't leave him behind. My mother would have taken him in, but I needed and wanted him on this journey.

Since the cabin was located in a remote wilderness area, the administrator thought it would be a good thing for Rambo to accompany me.

"There is no mention about dogs on the contract," she told me in the lyrical mountain twang I came to know well. "So bring him with you, sweetheart. I can't wait to meet him."

I'm Southern and more than accustomed to endearments like *honey* and *sweetheart*. In fact, I use them myself, but this was my first experience with East Tennessee's conversational sweet talk. I thought she was charming, especially after she gave permission for Rambo to accompany me, and I caught myself listening to every word that dripped off her tongue.

My mom helped me with the yard sale after I let the apartment go. Letting go of my possessions proved more emotionally difficult than I expected, so I kept more than I originally planned. I kept those crazy little Mexican chairs, the braided rug, my iron bed, the green Mexican glassware, my Thai rubbing print, Granddad's rocking chair, and the afghan my grandmother made for my college graduation. The rest of it went home with others or to local charities.

I was surprised when Jason stopped by. After making sure Rambo was secure, he browsed and even bought a few things, but I seriously had to wonder if he was there to flirt with my mother. If so, to her credit, she was the perfect mom that day and was having none of it. Rambo, an impressive presence in his blue harness, refused to allow him to come near me.

Beyond a brief twinge of guilt over our parting, I felt virtually nothing when I saw him, not even when that stubborn jet-black curl slid onto his brow. Somehow the glamor that held me to him had faded to a dim memory. He was no longer my Prince Charming, just a vain man who had taken what was offered and then played me like a harp. A burden lifted from my shoulders when the stuff was all gone, and that included him.

I'd not seen my sanctimonious friend Cassie since that night at the Asian Fusion restaurant, nor had I given her much thought since then. Still, it came as a surprise when I realized that I had pulled away from her as well. What was going on with me?

On the eve of my departure, it was time for the proverbial mother/daughter conversation. After all, nobody knew me better than she, and who else but my mom would tell me the unvarnished truth and then set me off on the journey?

Storing what I had decided to keep at her place, Rambo and I stayed there just prior to leaving. This gave us about a week to catch up. Just before I left, we took a bottle of wine and Mom's best pink crystal goblets out to the deck where we sat listening to frogs and crickets, watched the fireflies and bats, and talked well into the night.

"You are so like me and yet so different," she said, cuddling up to a befuddled Rambo who didn't yet know how to take her affection. "When your dad died, and I resumed life among the living, I realized many of the things we shared still had power over me and that I needed to let them go. The transition was a painful process. Somehow, I don't think you even needed to think about it. You've gotten rid of the old baggage and picked up the new without a second thought, haven't you?"

Astounded by my mother's astute observation and the comparison between us, I stared at her, my mouth hanging open. She's always been like that—almost psychic. It's like she can read my mind before I know what I've thought about. It can be downright discomfiting to have someone see your inner-most thoughts like that. This time, the door for discourse opened wide as we discussed what holds us back, and how we allow others to shape our opinions until we've had enough. While I am not a replica of my mom, it pleased me that in those ways I am like her. It's because of her that I finally discovered how to put that oppressive voice from my father to rest, remembered the good times, and then moved on.

"He really was a good man, Marianna; don't ever forget that. He loved us both dearly, but he did what was needed then. This is now," she reminded me sternly. "Move on."

The next morning's air was gray with dense fog, hot, heavy, and sticky with high humidity—the stuff Florida's bright, cheery tourism brochures ignore. Water dripped off every surface, and my hair fell the minute the damp hit it, but I took it in stride knowing a bad hair day to be a small price to pay for freedom. We didn't have a whole lot to do since I'd loaded the Subaru the night before.

Leaving mom peering teary-eyed through the screen door, I walked briskly down the path lined with colorful caladiums and giant elephant ears without looking back. The minute the door opened, Rambo leaped into the passenger seat, did his rotation thing, and settled himself on his favorite pillow and blanket, ready to ride.

I turned back to see that Mom had changed her mind and followed me out to the car after all. I hugged her one more time, got in next to the Rambo and tried not to look behind me when we drove away. We headed down the twisting avenue of ancient live oaks dripping with moss and showy Camellia bushes filled with rich pink blossoms with more bravado than I really felt. I knew my mother was still watching when I turned the corner and could see her no more, but we were blasting into the future, and there was no turning back.

We cleared Thomasville, Georgia, with its aura of old money but soon after, the landscape took on a monotonous sameness. It seemed the trip through south and middle Georgia's farmland took forever. On second thought, the trip through Georgia does take forever, due in part to the fact that there's no relief on the landscape or rest for the emotions of the susceptible—miles of farm fields and old towns filled with older memories perpetuated by thoughts that cannot die. Soon, I wanted to find a way over, under, or around the sameness of it, but there was no way to go but through. Once we hit I-85 for the drive through Atlanta, there was little time to think with multiple lanes of traffic racing for first place.

This was our first real road trip as Rambo was just now travel-worthy. He needed to stop periodically as did I, and that we managed, but finding safe places to leave him in the car were few for a lone driver.

We pressed on, my dog and I, until we cleared the heavy truck traffic of Atlanta, leaving congestion behind for broader spaces and a rolling hilly landscape. Pushing into North Georgia, things got much better. We saw our first mountain, and our surroundings turned a rich forest green. A great lump formed in my throat at the sight, especially when I saw the bluish haze rising in the distance.

Ever aware of my emotions, Rambo's big pointed ears perked up. He stared out the window like a fully sentient being, which perhaps he really was. Not long after, the little Subaru took to the mountains like a goat. We flew through Toccoa, past Tallulah Falls, Clayton… and then into North Carolina's Balsam, Brevard, Dillard, and Sylva where fall's first sentinel—bright yellow Goldenrod—lined the highways. It is said that one can get sick from too much beauty, and I believe you can; it took all I could do to keep the car on the road there was so much to see.

Giddy from otherworldly beauty, and hungry, we pulled into a motel just outside of Asheville before sundown. I was tired of driving and wanted to be wide-awake and fully aware when we drove over Sam's Gap and Bruckner's Pass.

Shimmering dew clung to the trees when Rambo and I set out on the last leg of our journey the next morning. It was exciting for a number of reasons—as a child when my family took vacations in the Southern

Highland Mountains, Mom and Dad always sang portions of the Hallelujah Chorus as we passed through the majestic Appalachian Mountains. Thank goodness some things never change. There were awe-inspiring vistas in every direction no matter what time of the year we drove it or how many times we did it.

This time was no different; as far as the eye could see, mountains rose in surreal harmony with one another. Even the roadway cutting through them failed to diminish the impact of their glory. It seemed as though they would go on forever, but finally, I realized we were descending into the valley while those rich green mountains, still a mighty presence, were further away.

The familiar and treasured rite of passage accomplished, I turned at the Elizabethton, Tennessee, exit, taking the road to journey's end, Roan Mountain.

Beyond stiffened legs each time we got out of the car, the still-healing Rambo took to the road like a champion. At rest stops, he stayed close by my side almost guarding me. In return, I watched him for signs of discomfort, stopping frequently to allow him necessary exercise. Not that he asked for it. Rambo seemed content on his side of the car as long as he could touch me with his big black nose, or place a paw on my leg.

"You doin' alright, Mr. Rambo?" I cooed like a silly goose. He lifted his head just enough to gaze into my eyes with something very much like worship. "I've got to make a pit-stop, okay? You'll get out to make a pee, too, and do some rompin' and checkin' out all the other dogs who've been here before us. Are you ready, big boy?"

He flicked his ears at that. I know, I know. I was speaking to him like he was a child, but at times, his magical blue eyes reflected what I swear was understanding. Such was our deepening bond that I could not help myself. Besides, my dog was never critical of me.

We began the gradual ascent that took us to the ridges, peaks, coves, and grassy *Balds* that are a part of the Southern Highland Mountains. Businesses thinned out, and homes grew farther apart until it was mostly highland vegetation and forest. I stopped at a tiny mom-and-pop restaurant in the small town of Roan Mountain, picked up burgers, and kept going. Then we made our way up to Tennessee's highest peak.

I wanted to be installed in our temporary home by full dark but the trip up the divided mountain took longer than anticipated. Driving up and around the mountain's steep incline on miles of switchbacks on steep and winding roads, I worried the radiator would blow. It was with relief that we finally reached the ranger's outpost to pick up the key and get directions to the cabin.

Staff were closing up for the day but took the time to give me literature, instructions, and warnings aplenty. Huge parts of the mountain really are true wilderness, and they made sure that I was fully aware of the dangers I might encounter.

Yes, there were black bears in abundance that year, but mast of acorns from the tree cover was plentiful for them. Still, they warned me never leave food out where wild animals could gain access, to always place garbage in covered, secured bins, that I should not look a bear straight in the eye, and not to run… on and on it went. Honestly, in my eagerness, most of it passed me by.

"Listen, guys," I said, glancing up at the sky, "That sun is sinking fast, and I need to get settled before dark. Is there anything else that I absolutely need to know before we head up there?" There was no mention of wolves, though one of the rangers showed discomfort when he saw my dog. The significance of his unease failed to register until much later.

"He's part wolf, wouldn't you say?" he said to one of the other rangers. Then looking at me he added with a chuckle, "Too much dog for a woman her size, wouldn't you say?" I heard the comment, so to waylay further speculation, I told them about how he came into my life, introducing him as a purebred white German Shepherd.

"There's still some wolves on the mountain," one of the men insisted on telling me, "but they shouldn't give you any trouble, 'specially not durin' the daytime, ma'am. Just you keep that collar and the harness on your dog and make him stay on a leash when you're out, and you'll be okay. This isn't the place for a new dog to run loose."

Leaving the rangers standing outside the station, the key and directions to the cabin in hand, I felt like we had made friends until out of the corner of my eye, I noticed one man who stood apart, watching us.

He was the one from which Rambo had kept a cautious distance from since the minute we arrived; the same one who'd expressed concern about his looking like a wolf. Eager to get to my new home, I pushed this observation to the back deck of my mind and drove on, but something about him filed itself quite firmly in my mind. Was it his stance, cocky and solidly built, or the hat tilted at an angle in defiance of the status quo?

Anticipation building by the second, I forgot the ranger when we again took to the road, driving around and around on the narrow road, going ever higher, seeking a barely visible metal marker that led off-road onto a graveled track. That was my first experience of driving up the mountain at sunset and on gravel. While I never came to love the crunchy stuff, I had to admit that it aided the tough little Subaru's traction on a couple of steep turns.

Even with a map, finding the cabin took some real detective work. The sun always sets early in the mountains so it was almost down when I saw the sign and we turned onto the dirt track that led us to our new home. Framed by ancient poplars, giant red and white oaks, and maples, and practically hidden from the narrow lane, the tiny cabin proved to be picture perfect. Diminutive from the outside, the log and mortar cabin with its high-peaked roof and charming front porch seemed to waver before my eyes, almost as though by enchantment. Long arching branches overhung the porch. Emblazoned on the porch support was the ancient Greek symbol for Chi Roe or good fortune. Finding it oddly familiar and strangely out of place, I promised myself to look into its significance at some point in the near future, but meanwhile, I wanted to explore the cabin.

Entering through the heavy scarred door made from one thick slab of wood, I discovered an interior which consisted of a great room with wide, deep windows, a big fireplace, and a spacious bedroom with a walk-in closet adjacent to the bathroom. There were high, open-beam ceilings with paddle fans, plus central heat and air should it be required. A partially enclosed deck in the back overlooked the gorge and the mountains of East Tennessee and North Carolina. Next to the coffee pot was a letter of welcome from the grant administrator, with numbers to call and a wish for good luck.

And speaking of luck, I was really glad the fiercely protective Rambo was with me, a fact which admittedly had settled some fears among my friends and especially my mother. No sooner had we entered the cozy cabin than he mounted an investigation of our surroundings, searching every nook and cranny of it. Satisfied we had the place to ourselves he sealed the deal by settling on the thick braided rug in front of the fireplace. That became his special place for the duration of our stay while I preferred the comfy soft leather chair to the side of it. Opposite from mine was a massive affair crafted out of weathered leather. It was fit for a full-bodied Sasquatch and much too big for my comfort. Before the night was fully settled, my grandmother's afghan lay across the back of that mama-bear chair, and one of her soft old quilts awaited me on the bed. I had come home.

That first night on the mountain I spent in an exhausted dreamless sleep. The next morning both Rambo and I awoke eager to see what our new world had to offer. Inhaling crisp air frosted with hints of fall's first breath, we took a walk, and then I finished unpacking the car, stocking the shelves and closet with the few possessions and clothes that I brought with me. After setting up my workstation, we set out to explore the magical woods immediately surrounding the cabin.

My teaching sessions at Cloudland Community Center, scheduled to begin the first week in September, gave me time to explore at leisure. Though the lush magenta rhododendrons were long gone, summer's aging beauty was perfect. I took to the wild like a deer in heat and that green realm embraced my desire.

Warm days found us exploring the Appalachian Trail with other hikers, learning the trail marker placements and finding animal paths in the woods. We had been in residence for less than a week when a knock at the door set Rambo off and scared me out of at least a year's growth.

Peering out of the front window, I saw a man I didn't know leaning against the porch rail, apparently in a good deal of pain. Grabbing

Rambo's harness, I opened the door. Had he been able to run, that man would have when he saw my dog.

"Excuse me, ma'am, I'm harmless. I promise! Please don't let that dog loose," he said, backing up. Then he showed me a card bearing the same Chi-Rho sign as that on the porch. "I think I've got a bad sprain; can you help me?"

It turns out he was an Appalachian through-hiker who knew the cabin's location by the symbol. I knew then I would have to find out more about it because at that moment I felt like a sitting duck.

While I helped the hiker, I grumbled under my breath. The residency sponsor should have told me about this sort of thing, especially if it was going to be a regular happenstance.

The cabin was stocked with an emergency kit, so with Rambo on guard, I strapped a stretch bandage around the ankle, drove the Subaru to the front porch and then ferried the man down to the ranger station. I felt quite proud of myself and grateful for Rambo's presence that day but I never quite got over the fear I felt at opening the door to strangers. Fortunately for me, it only happened that one time, but I thought about it each time I opened that heavily scratched front door.

I also questioned who or what made those scratches... a bear?

Most evenings I spent wrapped in a blanket out on the deck watching the sunset, or recording my impressions by lantern-light with Rambo at my side. Rainy days found me hibernating, reading books that I'd not taken the time to read in the past. Fortunately for me, whoever stocked those shelves knew my reading tastes well.

With cooler nighttime temperatures, scents of spruce tangled with wild honeysuckle lingered in the air, mixing with wood smoke drifting up from below us. That and the scent of frying bacon awakened something primeval and restless in me, but I couldn't figure out why.

After all, I had meaningful work, a good dog, a beautiful place from which to create and few distractions. The Internet reception was spotty—for a reliable signal I had to go down to the Cloudland Library a couple of times a week just to communicate with the outside world, but I didn't mind. In that kind of seclusion, ideas long suppressed spilled out of my fingers. It seemed that my work began to achieve a sharper edge with each session at the keys.

Eventually, I discovered that solo adventures had downsides. As Cassie predicted, I finally got lonely. My sessions were scheduled to begin the next Tuesday, so by that time I was primed and ready to jump into the fray.

Tuesdays were busy for me at Cloudland Community Center with teaching writing classes during the day, followed by a community, covered-dish supper after. Ten eager students greeted me in our classroom, beginning at 2:00 p.m. and adjourning at 5:30 p.m. Needing to get back to Rambo, I had not planned to stay for supper, but one of the participants, Nell Rogers, quickly introduced me to everyone before I left.

"Listen up, you'ns. This is our resident scholar, Marianna Ross. She's Christo's writer. She's gonna ask you for interviews about your family history on Roan Mountain. Stop by and talk to her pretty quick; she's new to these roads and needs to leave before it gets dark."

Christo's writer? I thought to myself, surely she didn't mean Christopher Papadis. The thought passed quickly as I met people and tried to register their faces and names.

Before leaving I had met almost everybody. Instead of the famed Appalachian reticence about talking to outsiders, my project was welcomed, and several residents signed up for interviews the next week. Such was Nell Roger's influence in the community and that of someone named *Christo*.

Thursday dawned crisp with more than a hint of fall in the air. Rambo and I were just coming in from our morning hike when a bright red pickup truck pulled into the yard, stopping behind the Subaru. Of course, Rambo immediately went into protection mode—someone had dared intrude on his territory.

The driver wisely waited until he calmed down to get out. "So this here's the white dog folks are talkin' about," Nell said in the southern highland dialect I would soon get to know much better. "He's a fine lookin' animal; that's for certain."

42

Glad for the company I welcomed her to my temporary home and walked over with him to greet her. "Rambo, this is Nell. She's a friend."

In response, he cocked his head, smelled her proffered hand, and then gave her a genuine tail wag.

"That's better! Come on in, Nell. We've just been out for our morning walk, and I'm ready for some coffee. I'm going to make a fresh pot, and I'd love some company. What's going on?"

In no time at all, I could see the wisdom of getting to know Nell Rogers went far beyond acquiring a new friend and getting some interviews. For one thing, she could trace her ancestry to the first settlers who found paradise in Appalachia. She was also key to the creation of my project; it was her proposal to the Lord Papadis Foundation that brought me to the mountains.

Before she left, Nell paused to say, "Now, you just come on down to the Community Center this Friday night and have some fun. I'll introduce you to more of the folks, and you'll hear real mountain music and, if we're lucky, some good storytellin,' too."

Something in my face must have shown concern because she added, "Don't you worry, child. There'll be other newcomers like you. It may be that some Appalachian Trail hikers will join us, too. They're almost always good folks."

I had mixed feelings about accepting her invitation: I didn't know those twisting roads with their hairpin turns and switchbacks, and dreaded driving on them at night. But I was lonely; the prospect of meeting new people was appealing, especially if some of them were potential interviewees.

Chapter 5

Late Friday afternoon, the invigorating chill of a cold front combined with the full moon drove me out of the house and down the mountain. Excited, I decided to pretty-up a bit, going so far as to wash and blow dry my hair and adding a bit of makeup before leaving. Rambo, entrusted with watching over the cabin, barely batted an eye when I left.

The trusty forest green Subaru, transformed into a magical fairy carriage for the night, spirited me down the mountain without a single mishap.

As promised, Nell waited at the door to greet me. "I'm proud you came down here to meet with us instead of foolin' around at the cabin just thinkin' about it," she said with a grin. "Some folks get a fright from driving that road at night and then havin' to meet a bunch of us fierce mountaineers all in one place."

She had me there; she'd known all along that I feared that drive. Grinning, she turned to the assembled crowd to introduce me.

"This here is Marianna Ross from the Residency Program," Nell said in the twang that tickled my ears. "We chose her from a long list of folks who wanted to come here and write up our stories, and now she's here. Make her welcome!"

And make me welcome they did. Before it was over, I had been hugged and called sweetheart and honey. My hand ached from shaking so many of theirs. How I would ever remember their names I had no idea, but one thing I knew, I would keep the cadence and the sound of their voices in my mind and heart forever.

When the people I had come to meet turned back to their own friends and families, I suddenly felt unsure of myself and very much alone-an outsider. Everything changed when Nell found me lurking on the perimeter. She refused to allow me to hang back and drew me into a group of her friends. Sitting in their midst, listening to their chatter, I was completely enchanted, hanging onto every word and listening to the bluegrass band tune up. Things heated up considerably when they began to play, but that's also when I got worried.

Always a poor dancer, my dad accused me of having two left feet. I tried to avoid it until an old codger who didn't care what I wanted insisted on dragging me to the floor. Laughing the whole time, we stepped on one another's feet as we danced, and I began to relax. Later on, gossiping with the women around tables laden with goodies, I told them about myself, and even held babies, whatever came my way. until I locked eyes with one of the men in the Appalachian Trail maintenance

Everything changed when I locked eyes with one of the men in the Appalachian Trail group who was dancing with a local woman. Seeing them dancing near us, Nell called out to him. Still holding my eyes with his, he responded then danced away. My heart racing 90 miles a minute, I turned to back to Nell. "Who is that?" but she was already speaking with someone else.

Trying hard not to look conspicuous, it took all I could do to avoid staring at the man. One of my students, Sally-Ann Olson stopped by to chat and that helped, but it took a major effort to pull myself out of the enchantment he cast.

"So you like the view, do you?" Sally-Ann said with a knowing grin when I dragged my eyes to hers. "Don't worry, you're not alone. We all enjoy watching Christo dance."

Laughing, we agreed to meet for coffee after our writing session the next week. When she walked away, I had that ancient preternatural feeling that someone was watching me. Looking up, I stared straight into the midnight-blue eyes of the man they called Christo. I could swear he was planning to ask me to dance but never got a chance to find out.

Instead, a woman sitting directly behind me joined him on the dance floor.

Oh, shit, he didn't want to dance with me. He was looking at her!

I watched them dance for a while, thinking how it would feel to dance close to that lean body and to have those muscular arms wrapped around me, but then I shrugged it off. I wasn't a good dancer, and he obviously was; I would probably have embarrassed myself. It was getting late anyway, and finding the room suddenly stuffy, I rose to leave.

Saying goodbye to the few people I knew, I cut through the crowd, pausing only to acknowledge the mounted black bear looking down at me. From his perch, atop a display case, the bear dominated the hallway. How could anybody kill one of those majestic creatures? I thought to myself.

From that day forward I pondered the fate of the bear each time I passed it, wondering why it wasn't in the case instead of being on top of it but I never got to the root of it.

Turning away, I was getting into the Subaru when a bright shaft of light spread out across the parking lot. Turning back, I could see the tall figure of a man silhouetted in the doorway. "Hey, wait. Please don't go yet. I want to talk to you."

I knew instinctively it was the man I'd fantasized about earlier. In an odd piquant, I ignored his call and kept moving. Pulling out of my parking spot, I saw his frustrated, tall form backlit against the Community Center sign.

What did he want from me, and why was I running from him? Did I fear that my carriage might turn into a pumpkin with four mice running amok?

That night, I had trouble sleeping as images of the man stirred emotions I thought thoroughly tamped down. Instead, visions of smoldering eyes and a lean body lingered.

***

Christopher Papadis stood at the door watching until Marianna's tail lights disappeared in the darkness. "Who is that woman, Nell?" he asked when she joined him. "I tried to dance with her, but Stella interfered as usual."

"Christopher Papadis, you really don't know who that woman is? That's your new resident scholar, Marianna Ross," she said.

"What? Why didn't you tell me?"

"Son, how could I know you two had not met already? This is the first time I've seen you since you came home," she fussed back at him. "By the way, what did you do to make her clear out like that?"

"That's just it, I don't know." He looked downcast for a moment before looking down at Nell with a baleful gaze. "It was a new experience really. I've never had a woman run away from me."

Nell cackled at that and shot him a sideways glance. He ignored her and, instead, turned in the direction his scholar had gone. So Marianna Ross had his attention, Nell thought. This would stand watching.

*****

The oral history project proceeded nicely as early fall brought chilling rain, blustery days, and then bright colors to the mountains. Reticent at first, descendants of the early pioneers gradually opened up to allow their stories to be recorded. Some of their stories were so vivid and packed with detail that it was hard to believe they'd taken place in the late 1700s and early 1800s.

When I asked Nell about it, she reminded me of what the people of Appalachia call "going back."

"They reach back into their memories for objects, like Granny's blue, salt-glaze milk pitcher. Then they search their memories for the events surrounding that pitcher and pretty soon, Granny's story about the day the pitcher broke comes to life," she told me. "After that, it's oral history. We've dug up a lot of old stories around here that way, and that's what you're hearin'. I just hope that by recordin' those stories they don't forget the old ways of keeping 'em alive."

47

In my eagerness to capture their stories, I'd not thought of what the cultural impact might be. "But Nell," I said, "didn't ya'll ask me to do this. Should we stop?"

"No, girl. With folks movin' around nowadays and youngsters leavin' the mountains for work, we need to make sure there's more than one way to remember our stories. We have to do this or they'll be lost."

I wasn't completely convinced by Nell's logic, but I wanted to preserve the stories I'd heard since coming to Roan Mountain, so the project continued.

The Appalachian Trail passed half a mile from the cabin, providing opportunities for frequent exploration. If the weather was good, my free days were spent outside with Rambo at my side. On occasion we did day treks on the AT, meeting other hikers along the way.

Thoughts of the man called Christo from the community center frequently intruded on my woodland reveries. Would I see him again? Probably not. More than likely, he was well on his way toward trail's end on Mt. Katahdin in Maine. It was just as well; I had work to do. A man in my life at this point would be a major distraction, but I couldn't get him off of my mind.

Most days, on returning to the cabin from rambles in the woods, invigorated and imagination piqued, I worked next to the wide double windows overlooking the gorge. With few distractions, the laptop worked overtime. Sensations experienced in the wild fell from my fingers into short stories, prompting a burgeoning body of work.

Approaching the end of the residency's second month, I began to feel an impending sense of loss because I was in love with the place and its people and didn't want to leave. Too, invigorated by falls' crisp, cooler weather, it took all I could do to settle down to the laptop and try to work. Hettie, one of my oral history subjects who said she'd seen the signs for change in the weather, warned me about early snow, urging me to stock up on supplies. Thinking it was some old wives' tale from way back, I ignored her. Surely, I'd be back home in Florida by the time it snowed.

Sitting under the stars on our nice, safe deck with Rambo at my side, I could see the dark shadows of Mounts Mitchell, Beech, and

Grandfather in the distance. When a wolf howled in the distance my domesticated dog lifted his head, pointed his long muzzle to the sky, and responded with the most surreal, primitive sound I had ever heard. It sent chills racing from the top of my head to my toes, sounding so age-old and eerie.

I stared at Rambo in astonished wonder. I'd not heard him howl like that. When the haunting sound died away in his throat, he looked embarrassed himself. His comical expression made me wonder if he'd never done it before and was just as surprised as I. That wasn't the only time he emitted such a sound during our time on Roan Mountain, but I never forgot the howling response it drew from all around us on that tall mountain that evening. It sounded like there were hundreds of wolves up there, and I, the lone human, could only pretend it didn't bother me.

Almost in fear I stared at my beloved Rambo and wondered again, who are you?

Often, screech-owls serenaded me to sleep, their thin, high, warbling voices sweet on the mountain air, but on occasion the high-pitched hoots of the Northern Saw-whet Owl's too-too-toos kept sleep at bay. At daybreak one morning, sleep eluded me due to one of those birds. Unable to tolerate the bed a minute longer, I rose early. Anxious to get on with the day, and hoping to see one of those tiny owls in its habitat, I let Rambo out for his run instead of going with him. That's when I discovered just how much all the exercise we'd been getting benefitted him.

No sooner had I opened the door than he dashed out, nose to the ground. Before I could grab the harness, he lit out on a scent trail that took him out of my line of sight in seconds. I grabbed the first things that came to hand, my tall staff and his leash, and then took off after him. I found him an hour later, barking in full voice at the foot of a huge poplar tree. Keeping one eye on the prize and one on me, he circled the tree, prancing.

Muscles twitching, a cougar sat halfway up the tree on a thick branch with a small deer under its broad paw, long tail swaying in early morning's sunlight.

49

First snowfall came just before Thanksgiving. In spite of Hettie's warning, it caught me by surprise.

After teaching one last class on behalf of the grant I decided to take a hike up to the grassy bald summit with Rambo. Leaving at daybreak the next morning, I began the day in layers but by mid-morning, the jacket was tied around my waist when we approached the pinnacle. By noon, we were working our way back down, having passed the ancient rhododendron gardens when heavy, dark clouds once far away in the distance moved in. Alarmed, I set my eyes for home with Rambo taking the lead. We were already too late. Cursing myself for a fool when it began to snow, I was angry for being off-guard, but who could blame me? I grew up in Florida where snow is rare as hen's teeth.

Going from temperate to near freezing in a flash, the weather changed faster than I could adapt. Heavy clouds soon encased us in a dense shroud through which one could barely see.

I was not dressed for what we were to encounter. Even though I pulled the jacket on and the hood up, sliding cold hands into fleece gloves I kept in the pockets, my teeth chattered unchecked. Even Rambo acted like he was cold, keeping close by my side.

Having trekked the area several times, at least I knew the ridges and most of the remote areas pretty well, but that was in summer. Unfortunately, lowering clouds obliterated familiar mountain ranges in the distance as snowfall quickly cloaked my landmarks. With Rambo pulling hard at the harness, I set my walking staff for home, trying to walk at a brisk pace.

Soon the fleece jacket was coated in white, while underneath, the thick flannel shirt, already dampened from physical exertion, and the thermal underneath were soaked. My teeth continued to chatter uncontrollably, but it was my eyes that were most concerning. I pulled the stocking cap down over my eyebrows that helped protect them.

Breathing soon became a chore as ice-cold air seared the delicate tissues in the nasal cavities, forging frigid channels down my throat and into my chest. Ever my protector; the snow-white Shepherd slowed to nudge my leg every so often to keep me going when I wanted to stop. It helped me to stay focused since this was not my natural habitat. I was nervous and unsure of myself, and that made me clumsy.

As the landscape grew increasingly foreign, punishing cold began to take its toll. The words of a wise Native American came back to haunt me. "People have frozen to death up here in summer—always take caution." Well, I had thrown his wisdom to the winds unheeded. It was late fall, and we were in trouble. Had Rambo not been so determined to keep me moving, I'm sure I would have become a statistic.

Between the two of us, we slipped, slid, and skidded our way over rocks, downed trees, broken limbs, and new ice lurking beneath the wet snow. I was grateful we were going across the ridge and down, not climbing.

Catching a faint scent of smoke and then sighting sputtering smoke just over the last rise I cried, "It's our place, Rambo—let's go." Together, we battled the now alien terrain to reach the cabin, fear of falling replaced by concern for our home.

The first thing I saw when we made the clearing were big, humanoid tracks—a Yeti? Surely not...

I soon realized the fresh prints were from snow boots, appearing to belong to one person, but for a moment there, I believed the old legend about the wild-eyed mountain man. Then reality set in. Experienced hikers would have sought safety long before, as I should have done, so who was in the cabin?

Drawing around to the side of the cabin to come in at an angle, I got another surprise; a Ford F150, its shiny black finish already coated with the white stuff, was parked behind my Subaru. Inwardly, I groaned. The handgun and the pepper spray were stored inside the cabin, not on my careless person. A fat lot of good it did to have them inside the house.

Shivering uncontrollably now that I wasn't slipping and sliding down the slope, I signaled Rambo, who was eager as I to see who was there, to stay down and quiet. I crept to the window like a stalker instead of up the snow-covered front steps into who knew what.

To my astonishment, inside the cabin, all was cozy as could be. A roaring blaze in the fireplace made me feel the frigid temperatures

51

outside even more. The question foremost in my mind was who is in my house?

A dark-blue, hooded anorak hung on the coat tree next to mine. Huge snow boots stood on the rug by the door. Two slender male feet in warm wool socks rested on the hassock in front of what I thought of as the papa-bear chair. Suddenly, the issue became one of who was sitting in the big chair.

I couldn't take it anymore. I stomped around to the front of the house with Rambo barking and dancing by my side. Heedless of the danger with unreasonable anger supplanting fear, I skidded up the icy steps hanging onto the guardrail to keep from falling.

Pushing the heavy wooden door open with a vehemence that I felt to my toes, I yelled as best I could, "Who are you, and what are you doing in my house?"

Without getting up or moving anything more than his glittering navy blue eyes, the man looked up at me and said calmly, "I could ask who barges into my house yelling outrageous demands, except I know who you are. I'm Christopher Papadis, and you must be my writer in residence. Knowing you to be new to the area, I came up the mountain to make sure you had the essentials for a storm."

Suddenly, I wanted to sit down but I couldn't find the chair. Christopher Papadis. Oh, my God. *His* writer in residence? The rest of what he said failed to register because now I recognized him from the Community Center as the man Sally called Christo. The man who tried to speak to me and whom I ignored!

His eyes raked me from head to toe as he waited for me to process that bit of information, missing nothing. Satisfied that I had it figured out, he then disengaged from my grandmother's afghan to stand on long legs leading down to those warm-looking, stockinged feet I had seen earlier. Then with an insolent grin and without apology, he added the ultimate insult.

"I confess myself a bit shocked. I was expecting little more than a frozen goose, but it's good you finally decided to come home. I was about to set out to find you."

Frozen Goose? Me? Infuriated, I wanted to say something snarky in response and be anything but welcoming. However, my mother's training came into play—no matter that I was discomfited—I shouldn't be angry at someone who wanted to help me. Thinking thus, I calmed myself down a few ratchets, finally growing sentient enough to be grateful that he bothered to check on me in the midst of a blizzard.

I was not, however, giving up. I stood mute, arms crossed over my chest while we stared at one another. Our stubborn face-off got Rambo worried. He barked and danced between me and the unmoving Papadis, breaking the tension when he pressed his huge damp body against my thigh and pushed, throwing me off balance and into my employer's arms. I swear if the damned dog could have purred at the result, he would have done so.

Cool as can be, Christopher Papadis carefully straightened me up then held me at arm's distance. "I'm sorry, Ms. Ross," he said towering over me. "The unspoken law of the mountain demands when a person caught in the wilderness is without shelter, they are free to seek and take it. While I was not lost or in danger, there was cause to think you might be, so I came up to check on you. Had you not returned when you did, I would have sounded the alarm.

"And just in case you missed it, there's a Greek Chi Rho symbol on the porch support. It's well-known to through-hikers who recognize the sign, but apparently, no one thought to tell you about it. In a way, I used it myself today since I could not find your trail in the new-fallen snow and decided to wait for your return. Please accept my apology; it's no wonder that you were upset," he said, putting on his boots as he spoke.

By that time, what he was saying began to make sense, sending me into an advanced state of mortification. My teeth ceased chattering long enough to let me mumble something unintelligible, but then he resumed where he left off in an aloof tone of voice. "Now that I am certain you're safe, if you'll wait but a moment, I will go away and leave you and the dog to your happy isolation."

Dissatisfied with the direction things were taking, Rambo whimpered, watching us both with concern. While Papadis spoke,

Rambo again bumped his massive white head against my leg, demanding attention. His behavior deflated my angst and served to distract Papadis.

"Please accept my apology; it's no wonder that you are upset," he said, putting on his boots as he talked. "I'll call after the weather clears and perhaps, we can talk then."

Until that moment, my anger at his intrusion served to distract me from my nearly frozen state, but then my legs turned to jelly and my teeth resumed audibly clicking and clacking. Even poor Rambo was shaking, his steaming wet fur dripping on the floor. Willing myself not to cry, I turned to the crackling fire for solace.

Without another word, my unexpected guest segued into that of concerned helper. He went into the bathroom as though he knew the place by heart. Emerging with clean towels he gave one to me and then turned to my poor dog. He toweled Rambo as though he were a baby, and then led him over to the fireplace to dry. Meanwhile, toweled-dry, I huddled under a blanket in the mama-bear chair, trying without success to quell the chill that had overtaken my body. He hovered over me briefly, concern in his face, before retreating to the kitchen. He returned with fresh-brewed coffee in one of the dark blue mugs and put it into my cold hands. I tried not to cry, but the tears came anyway.

He watched in solemn silence as my emotions ran the gamut, flitting across my face like a movie trailer. Barriers relaxed, and I found myself embarrassed and yet profoundly grateful for his kindness. I managed a simple, "Thank you," with what little dignity I could muster, but I couldn't meet his eyes.

"Listen, Ms. Ross," he said, his midnight-blue eyes glittering, "If you stay in those damp clothes, you will get a chill. I mean you no harm but if you don't change into dry clothing, I will oblige on your behalf."

Instead of a snappy retort, I listened to the cool tones of his voice and heard the meaning in his words. Without saying a thing, I headed to my bedroom where I put on thick sweatpants, a warm and wooly sweater, and then added my favorite alpaca socks and fleece slippers. I even managed to run the brush through my hair and gargle with mouthwash before returning to the living room.

Feeling more myself, I scuffed over to my favorite place—the mama-bear chair with the stacks of books surrounding it—and settled in. Once there, he gently covered me with the big knitted afghan heated by his own body's warmth and the fire and then brought me yet another mug, this one filled with steaming hot tea dosed with honey.

Deflated by kindness, warmed by the fire and the tea, and no longer angry, curiosity penetrated my befogged brain.

Pouring himself another cup of coffee, he spoke with an old-world formality. "Do forgive the intrusion as it wasn't intended as anything beyond concern for your safety. Again, I am Christopher Papadis, Ms. Ross. Your residency sponsor. I'm also the man you ignored and ran away from at the Cloudland Community Center last month. If I may be so bold, I'd like to know why?"

Christopher Papadis... my residency sponsor. Also known as Christo! By this time, in an advanced state of mortification for thinking of how I had treated him and by the inescapable fact the man wasn't attracted to me that night, I wanted to hide. He just wanted to make contact with his employee.

"Oh, my gosh, Mr. Papadis," I stammered, stumbling over the words. "I didn't know. I'm so sorry. Please forgive me."

"There's nothing to forgive Ms. Ross. I regret not coming up to meet you sooner, but I was out of the country when you took residence. On my return, I joined my hiking group to do some trail maintenance up on the ridge. We usually plan our treks around getting to the Cloudland Center if we're still up there on a Friday night."

I understood little of what he was saying, since I was having trouble staying awake by then. The one thing I did understand was that I should have made better inquiries about my funding source. I sank even deeper into humiliation, missing most of what he said next. Then I caught the word "key."

"...and while I have a key," he continued, a somber look on his face, "I don't always visit the writers who come here during their stay. This time, however, since I am the sponsor of your residency, I felt some responsibility for your safety with a storm of this magnitude bearing down on the mountain." He cocked a dark eyebrow and looked at me with a critical eye. "Surely by now you can see I mean you no harm. Look at the way your dog acts with me."

Without saying another word, he sat across from me in the big papa-bear chair, crossed his arms, and prepared to wait for a response. My turncoat dog followed him. Collapsing at the man's feet, Rambo curled up and went to sleep with a silly grin on his face. I wish I could say the same. By that time, I was warm and wide awake.

Over six-foot, with hair the color of fine, dark chocolate worn on the long side, his eyes were the darkest blue I had ever seen. His skin was the color of dark honey and his teeth were incredibly white. With his slightly-crooked nose, square jaw, and archaic language, Christopher Papadis could have been a pirate for all I knew.

Mind you, I saw this without looking directly at him. In truth, it took all of my mother's strictest training—prior to her conversion to the bohemian lifestyle—in proper etiquette to avoid staring. I had been without a man far too long to be safe in the company of one as arresting as this one. Then I realized I was the ungrateful ragamuffin who'd just abused him so horribly. I wanted to say something but couldn't speak.

Most likely suffering from near hypothermia, in the absence of conversation, I dozed off still wrapped in my grandmother's handiwork with a delectable hunk of maleness sitting untouched across from me.

*****

Waking to silence the next morning with the sun glaring on the snow outside, my virtue—and considering my dreams, regrettably—intact, I discovered myself snug in my bed, still in the sweats from last night, under the down covers with Rambo curled by my side. Vague memories of being gently scooped up and carried off to bed rolled around in my foggy head, but I swear I couldn't recall anything more beyond some very sweet dreams.

The wet clothes I had on the night before were hung on the shower rod to dry—not my style either; I would have left them where they fell. Questioning this state of affairs, and having no idea what to say or do about my predicament, I padded into the kitchen in search of my drug of choice—caffeine.

My visitor was not in evidence, but the furnace was going, and the fire was ready for a match with a hefty stack of wood brought in to replenish the supply. In the kitchen, coffee was ready to start and next to the coffeemaker, was a neatly written note.

Ms. Ross,
Please accept my apology for barging into the cabin unannounced yesterday. By way of explanation, let me introduce myself again. I am Christopher Papadis, sponsor of the residency program. I usually introduce myself and make sure my writers have everything they need and always check in when inclement weather is predicted. My agent should have let you know that I was out of the country, but apparently failed to do so.
Again, forgive me for the rude surprise my presence gave you, but without a cell tower nearby, communication is limited and best left to chimney smoke and pigeons.
I will come again in a week to make sure all is well. Should you be able to come down the mountain before then and need to get in touch, call me at 395-2491. Until then, best regards,
CP

Strangely enough, a dramatic sense of letdown overwhelmed me when I read his note. It was too simple and straightforward, and too good to be true. It was surreal; there I stood "safe and sound" in my sweats with socks on my feet, hair sticking out in all directions, daydreaming about a mysterious dark stranger who had entered my life when I needed him most. It made no sense the night before and made even less now. Thinking the freezing cold would clear my befuddled thoughts, I stuck my head out the door to let Rambo go for his run on the long lead. The cold did nothing.

Listless all that day and the following, I sat bundled in my chair watching the snow pile up around the windows and huge icicles form on the eves. The landscape was surreal in its beauty. Every surface was layered in soft whiteness like the coat of a sleeping polar bear and almost completely silent. If a wilderness challenge was what I came here for, this was it.

Later in the day, I decided the experience of deep isolation would test my endurance skills. This would be the perfect time to finish the manuscript that I resurrected and brought with me. It had already languished untended for several years but unfortunately, would continue to do so for a while yet. Instead, trapped inside with the perfect situation in which to write, I couldn't concentrate. The laptop sat idle while I stared out the windows and daydreamed.

The next morning, I had a headache, and by mid-afternoon it became clear why I couldn't concentrate. I was coming down with something. My throat turned raspy, and by nightfall my chest felt like an elephant had stepped on it. When a rattling cough started, I made some hot tea, crawled into bed with a groan, and stayed there. Sickness, I was not prepared for.

The next morning, I woke with a raging fever in a dark, cold cabin. It soon appeared that fragile electrical lines snapped further down the mountain during the night, leaving us with no power. The fire was out and Rambo, who had crawled under the covers to find more heat, was hogging the space and most of the blankets. Fuzzy-headed and finding each breath a struggle, I donned ski jacket and hat, gloves, and boots, and headed out to the woodpile just outside the door. Birds searching for bits of food rose as Rambo dashed into their midst, startling them into the air, on his mug a happy smile.

The world had turned even more densely white overnight, with every tree etched in white, trimmed with icy lace. Enormous ice and snow sickles suspended from the roof like long fangs, but I was too sick to enjoy the beauty. Had I been completely conscious, the pleasure of being in it would have been supreme.

Calling the dog inside was not an easy task. Rambo loved to play in the snow. In addition, he knew my limitations and played them well. The harness and leash were helpful, but only so far as I had the strength and determination to wield them.

Freezing cold chilled the exposed skin on my face, tearing at each breath. In a panic and frightened when I could barely see his white coat in the snow, I jerked the leash and called Rambo in a croaking voice. He came but it was with reluctance that he did it.

A normally obedient dog, Rambo almost always listened to me, but for the first time I saw the wild, unruly animal inside of him and feared to lose him to the wilderness. Then I saw the reason for his behavior; in the distance just beyond a heavily weighted clump of trees, something white moved out of sight. Just that fast he pulled hard against the leash. Caught off guard, I let go.

"Rambo, no!" I croaked, but he was already gone, and I could not follow him.

Struggling to stay on my feet I decided to let him take his own chances. It was either that or die, and I knew it. I'd just barely made it up the steps, then mournfully turned to shut the door, when to my happy surprise, he nosed his way past me.

Blue eyes dancing merrily, Rambo pranced all around the big room, shaking his heavy coat with the greatest joy. His splashing everything in sight with ice water seemed to energize him even more while all I wanted was a tissue and the down comforter. Instead, I grabbed a towel and dried his wriggling body as best I could, haranguing him between hacking coughs.

"You are a naughty dog! I thought I'd never see you again!" The scolding apparently did nothing to lessen his enthusiasm because, with puppy-like eagerness, he bathed my face in slobbery kisses. Tears in my eyes, I sat on the floor holding him, drawing comfort from his solid, damp presence.

With Rambo settled, I made hot tea from the kettle on the fireplace grate and then crawled back in bed. Then I realized the fire was a mass of smoldering ashes. Groaning from the effort, I crawled out of bed once again and was about to head out to the woodpile when I spied the neat stack at the back door left by my thoughtful employer. I had been so sick I missed it, blearily walking right past it, in fact. The fire roaring once again, I lay back down to consider our encounter. It wasn't necessary for Christopher to have brought in that much wood or any of the other things he had done for Rambo and me. Grateful for his thoughtfulness, but also aware he knew it wouldn't look good if his writer froze to death, I wondered if anything would be expected in return.

The next day, rousing just enough to inspect my appearance in the tiny bathroom mirror, I saw dirty, stringy hair, a pale face, a red nose, and dull eyes peering back at me. The looking glass couldn't lie, so the truth I saw reflected there filled me with despair. I had gone rustic during this mountain retreat, but now, I looked absolutely deadly. Now, in addition to dark circles rimming my red, bleary eyes, my normally smooth skin was dry and patchy. My hair was out of shape, the color gone from carefully maintained soft honey-blond to unglamorous mousy brown. In just under three months of neglect, it was now a mess. My mother would have had apoplexy had she known a man of Christopher Papadis's caliber had seen me in such a state. Much less that he, a total stranger, had put me to bed, that he saw the untidy stack of clothes on the bathroom floor and hung them up to dry. Then a thought of far more serious import struck me. I devoutly hoped the underwear I had worn that day were some of my best. It was, unfortunately, too late to do anything about it. The damage, if there was any, was already done. Christopher Papadis probably saved my life, even though he had to do it without asking and with no assistance from me. But what did he think about what he saw? Oh, dear gods and goddesses, fates, muses, and whoever else I could think of, what was I supposed to do now?

By the third day, I was beyond caring. A searing cough had sunk so deep into my chest that it hurt to breathe. I couldn't bank the fire, hadn't eaten in two days and could barely make it to the bathroom sink for water or stagger to the back door to let Rambo out on the deck and to feed him. Was it pneumonia? Bronchitis?

When he wasn't asleep by my side or at my feet, Rambo began to whine. He paced the floor, going back and forth to the windows to peer at the winter-white world outside and then back to me. I finally took to putting him on the leash and letting him go out the back door on the deck with the end looped securely around the doorknob from the inside. It would have been a simple thing for him to break loose, but he didn't try. Even though his pent-up energy was building, it was all I could do for him. I was one sick puppy who desperately needed his presence and body warmth when he could be still long enough.

The fourth day, the electricity came on and the fridge activated. Those welcome sounds penetrated the mental fog, but it wasn't enough to rouse me from the stupor into which I had fallen.

When Rambo jumped off the bed and begged to go out, all I could think was, "Oh, dear Lord, he has to go out again." Snow was piled up halfway to the roof, making it more difficult to get the back door open for him. He stayed out just long enough to baptize the snow deep yellow and then gingerly pick his way back to me. Luckily, the pipes didn't burst.

Eventually, it became necessary to get more wood into the cabin for the fire. Blessed with southern exposure and free of the packed snow on the north-facing front porch, I could still open the door to the deck. It was a bright day with full sun so the deck snow was already melting. That's when I found yet another stack of wood under a tarp, right where it had been the whole time. I decided then and there that I was in love with Christopher Papadis though I barely knew him.

Feeling woozy but at least sentient, I made coffee for the first time in days. Inhaling the rich fragrance and welcoming the heat on my aching throat, I drank deeply from the elegant dark blue ceramic cup. That's when I noticed the logo imprint—Lord Papadis, Asheville, North Carolina—my landlord's company? Would wonders never cease?

Hunger lurking in the back of my mind caused me to search the cabinets for a can of soup—tomato preferably, but the larder was nearly empty. How could I have been so careless? Saltine crackers and coffee had to suffice for the time being and were perhaps the better choice anyway.

With caffeine kicking in and thinking much more clearly, curiosity about Christopher Papadis got the better of me. I took the laptop over to my favorite chair to do a bit of research. Sluggish at first from inactivity and intense cold, my lifeline to the outside world took its own sweet time to boot. Both the computer and I gradually warmed up, but my search bore no fruit; there was no internet—not even the fragmented kind. For the first time, I felt irritation at the limitations of living just beyond civilization.

Taking a hot shower, the first in days, and inhaling steam to clear my chest helped, but when I made a critical review of myself to see what kind of damage the past three days had done, I was appalled by I what found. Marianna Ross had definitely rusticated in her retreat from the world.

I had applied neither moisturizers nor sunscreens as I should have; my skin had roughened from being outdoors so much. The eyebrows definitely needed shaping and my hair was uneven. And my hands? Don't even go there. Add to that the ravages from fever and I was a wreck. It was time to venture down the mountain for the purpose of self-improvement.

I did what I could just in case Christopher Papadis elected to pay another visit, but I couldn't leave the cabin for several more days. The car was completely snowed over and looked like a small mountain. I had no spare energy to shovel my way out, so the only reasonable thing to do was to crawl back into bed, pile on more covers and try to get well. Surely, we'd have a thaw soon, and I could dig my way out then.

Sometime later in the day, Rambo set to barking at the window. Then I heard what I hoped was a Park Services snow plow coming up the mountain. A more welcoming sight I could not have asked for. Peering through the thick, ice-crusted glass, I saw a massive, dark navy-blue SUV with a plow affixed to the front forging a path through the snow straight to the cabin. When it stopped at my front door and the visage of Christopher Papadis emerged, my poor heart did a finely executed somersault. Already thinking of him as the prince of the mountain, I longed to run outside and throw my arms around his neck with reckless abandon. Instead, attempting to strive for a modicum of dignity, I tried to drag the thick door open, coughing with the effort when I heard him shout, "Stand back, Ms. Ross, let me do it. Hold the dog, please."

I did as he asked, holding a struggling Rambo as best I could. Had he really wanted to escape my arms he could have. Instead, he acted the clown, giving me a hard time in the process.

The minute the door opened, Rambo, knowing full well who it was, pushed past me and did what I wanted to do. A flash of pale on white snow, he ran, jumped, barked, and barreled around the man, running in circles while my benefactor stood there on the porch laughing at his antics. With boundless energy himself, Christopher called out a greeting to me and then proceeded to play with Rambo until the dog was exhausted. His every footstep followed closely by Rambo, Christopher then pulled numerous bags out of the extended cab, and made his way inside, sloshing through the rough path of frozen mush Rambo had made.

Striding up the steps two at a time with his arms filled with cloth grocery bags, Christopher entered the cabin as though he were indeed, King of the Castle. For that moment, he really was. Tall and darkly rugged, his presence commanded the room like that of a huge black bear. Cool as could be, I maintained a calm front, but inside I quivered with excitement. Here, in my living room was a real-life human being, and a helpful one at that.

During my illness, separation from society had begun to penetrate my psyche. If I learned anything from it, it was that I needed human companionship on occasion; at that very moment, my benefactor fit the bill perfectly. He was a charming hunk of humanity in his heavy wool fleece coat, black cap with earflaps, leather gloves, flannel lined jeans and thick-soled boots. When he took the coat off, it was to reveal a heavy, red-plaid flannel shirt. I've always had a weakness for men in flannel... It was worn over wool thermals that I could see peeking out at the neck. A full day's beard darkened square jaws; both primitive and intensely attractive, he loomed large in the little cabin like a god from Mt. Olympus.

Greetings accomplished, he proceeded to stock the larder, after which he turned those penetrating blue-black eyes on me. I was glad of the shower earlier in the day and happy that I was presentable this time around but an involuntary shiver ran up my spine. I could see him surveying every detail, including my beleaguered appearance, the piles of used tissue, unwashed cups, paper and books on the desk, with more stacked by my chair and lined up against the walls.

"You've been sick," this said in an unexpected tone of reproof. When he continued, there was tacit disapproval in his voice. "That you couldn't help, but your kitchen shelves were already nearly empty when the storm hit. There's no excuse for this kind of carelessness, Ms. Ross. Letting your food supplies run low up here is a foolhardy thing to do, especially this time of year. Don't you realize that if your illness had gone into pneumonia, both you and Rambo could well have starved to death? It's more than possible that nobody would have found you until some random hiker happened by!"

I recoiled at the severity of his words, but I could also hear the truth in them. Few people in my life have ever dared speak to me in such a way, but I had to admit that I was guilty of gross neglect. I failed to stock the pantry when I was hale and hardy. Add to that, I totally misjudged the weather and overrode my own symptoms, allowing both me and my dog to fall into a compromising situation. To say that I was embarrassed and wanted to hide is an understatement, but I had nowhere to go.

Christopher Papadis glared at me while I tried to find a rejoinder, but I had no words at my disposal. Unexpectedly, his expression reminded me of my old friend from Florida, the sanctimonious Cassie, and that tipped me into anger. My displeasure came out in my quick raspy retort.

"Look, Mr. Papadis, I'm just grateful to have survived this nightmare. Thank you for bringing supplies and for everything you've done for me, but while I've been stupid, and that I admit, you've no right to remind me of it. I'm not a child."

Something sparked in those midnight-blue eyes when his right eyebrow shot up to his brow-line

"You are most welcome, Ms. Ross. I try to take care of my resident scholars, even the ones who forget what time of year it is and what must be done to stay alive on this mountain when emergencies arise."

Stung by yet another rebuke, I remained silent when he went out to get more firewood. When he returned, I was ready with another pithy comment, but he beat me to it. Dragging the heavy gloves off of his hands, he turned a critical eye on me and then cocked an eyebrow.

"Well, I must say that in spite of everything, you clean up nicely." This he said with such a sardonic wolfish grin that again, I was flummoxed. Without another word, he turned to stoke the fire.

Robbing me of a shrewish response, my body betrayed me; I croaked and then coughed from my toes up. He stood back up and turned to me again, alarm in his eyes. "Seriously, just how long have you been like this?"

I tried to tell him, between coughs, but finally gave up. The effort of speaking was too much. All kindness now, he led me to my favorite chair, tucked me in, and then went into the kitchen to make tea.

Depressed, I thought that if he might ever be inclined toward attraction to me, I had just driven it clean out of his head. He was, however, clearly solicitous of my well-being, which eased those concerns only the tiniest fraction.

Stirring in a dollop of local honey, he brought the tea and then settled in the oversized leather chair. Unbidden the thought came to me that he had spent many hours in that chair in the past. Rambo immediately deserted my side and collapsed on the floor with a loud sigh between us and the fireplace.

"Poor Rambo," I said in a ragged, sotto voice. "He's been cooped up in here with me almost a week, only stepping out on the deck to do his business. While he's been good about it, he's miserable with all of that built-up energy."

"I can see that. If you want, I'll take him out for a quick run in a bit. That will take care of Rambo, but I really think that you need to see a doctor. I have a meeting in Elizabethton this afternoon; come with me, and I'll drop you at Urgent Care and then collect you after my meeting if you don't mind waiting. Would that help? What more can I do?"

Evading making a decision, I spoke instead to the needs of my dog. "It would help a lot if you'd take Rambo out," I responded. Hearing his name Rambo snapped to attention, looking hopefully at the door.

"As for taking me to the doctor, I don't want to put you to any trouble. If you'll clear the snow off of the lean-to, I'm sure the Subaru can make it down the mountain and back. Besides, I'm longing to get out of here, too. Poor Rambo and poor me—we are accustomed to being outside a good portion of every day. Being closed up like this has tested us both, especially him, though he's been good about it. Be careful, though. I think he is only a step removed from going wild. A wolf appeared not long after we got here. They've been communicating regularly ever since."

Nodding, he said, "It's wise to take care. You're not likely in danger from them since they generally live and let live unless they're starving. Rambo is another matter since, given the right circumstances, he might run off to join his wild friends."

He stared at Rambo for a moment and then added with his hand resting on the snowy white head, "He's certainly smart enough to be part-wolf," reminding me too much of what the sullen-looking ranger said when we first arrived.

I watched with a half-smile when Rambo settled his head on his big white paws, fantasizing what it would feel like to have Christopher's big hand on me. As a result, I was far from content.

The silence grew until I began to cough again, bringing attention back to my health. Christopher got me a glass of water and stood there towering over me. He was obviously pondering the situation because when he spoke, this time brooking no opposition.

"Come, I can see your concern about leaving your dog, but you must go to the doctor," he insisted. "Driving conditions are really bad right now with slick black ice in places. If you felt better and knew the bad spots, I'd not question your desire to drive yourself to Urgent Care, but you don't. I will take you, and Rambo will come with us."

Between coughs, I finally agreed. While he took Rambo out for a romp, I changed into heavy-weight winter gear, applied a bit of makeup to my poor parched face and in general, tried to make my sorry-self look presentable.

Thus, it was that Rambo ceded his shotgun seat to me, and rode in the backseat cab of the truck down 321 to Elizabethton. It was the first time we had been down the mountain since our arrival, and it couldn't have looked more different had we landed on the moon.

Every surface was covered in thick white layers of fresh snow. Here and there it had melted off of rooftops, but most houses were mounds of white with narrow tunnels dug to the front door. Spirals of smoke drifted aloft from chimneys barely visible from the road. Here and there I could see where herds of deer had walked across places I couldn't begin to think of trying.

On the drive down Roan Mountain, my sense of curiosity reawakened, and suddenly, I felt a strong need to know what was going on in the outside world. Then, in quick succession, it dawned on me that I had lost a week to illness and had only three precious weeks left in Tennessee to complete the narrative from my interviews.

It seemed that Christopher and I were thinking along the same lines. He turned to me and said, "One of the things we'll address at today's meeting is your work. The reports you've submitted are outstanding but it seems there are more areas to investigate. We are especially interested in the stories old Saul tells. You haven't interviewed him, have you?"

I shook my head in the negative and then listened in stunned silence as he continued. "You've been ill for a week and have also lost time to this storm. If you are willing to continue, I'd like to propose that you stay on until you have completed the project. Are you game?"

Was I game? All I could think of was, *Yes!* But I answered with as much decorum as a woman with a horrific cough could muster to whisper in the affirmative.

"Good," he said with a self-satisfied grin. "I was hoping you'd agree. I will see what I can do to make it happen."

I wanted to know about him. Thus began a simple interrogation of my benefactor, who, it seemed, was quite willing to answer my questions.

"It was you I saw at the Cloudland Community Center, wasn't it?" I asked him in my croaky voice. "You tried to tell me about it that day at the cabin, but I was so fuzzy that the connection didn't penetrate my poor brain. I also remember the Center's announcer said you all were working on the trail and had come down to take a break."

"Yes, I'm a member of a hiking group based in Woodfin, near Asheville, and we go up each quarter to spend a few days on trail maintenance. Sometimes we'll overnight and then go down to the

67

Cloudland Center for the music and storytelling. When I saw you there, I had no idea you were our resident writer. Tell me, why did you run away like that? Did you think I was a bear or an ogre for wanting to dance with the new girl in town?"

Embarrassed at the turn my interrogation had taken, I blundered around until I just had to quit and make a confession.

"Look," I said, with my eyes cast down to the floorboard, "I am fresh from a bad relationship and new to this area. When you started signaling me from the dance floor, I wasn't sure what you were trying to do or that it was even me you were trying to connect with. Frankly, it was confusing. Then there was this old guy in the white polyester leisure suit and long ponytail who kept sniffing around—I just didn't know what to do. I wanted to dance and might have done so had not that woman behind me jumped up. Then I was embarrassed, thinking it wasn't me you wanted at all. Besides, I saw that she was with your group earlier in the evening and didn't want to mess in somebody's pudding."

That brought a snuffling sound from my dog and a chuckle from my driver. With a gentle smile, he ignored my discomfort and then sketched a brief bio for me.

"First, I used to be involved with the woman but no more. It was awkward when she flung herself into my arms for the dance; the old guy comes from over the state line in North Carolina. He's a widower; he and his wife used to dance together until she died. He thinks he's a lady-killer in his eighties suit, but really, he's quite harmless and a pretty good dancer. The next time just tell him you don't want to dance or that all your dances are saved for me." This last he said with a wicked grin, and when I had the grace to actually blush, he changed the subject, keeping me occupied with stories about his family.

"My parents are from Greece, but I was born in America—Asheville to be specific," he continued, needing no prompts from me. "I am the second-born son of an olive oil manufacturing family who just happens to be royalty in the old country—hence the name of our company—Lord Papadis. My tutor was a Greek national educated in Boston. He raised me as an international with both English and Greek as my languages. With dual citizenship, by the time I came of age, I spoke both languages as a native. Now I travel back and forth several times a year, but America is far more home to me than Greece. My family's only disappointment is that I never married a nice girl from the homeland. God knows they've tried hard enough. I've dated a fair number of women, but never found the one I wanted to make my wife and life partner."

His family's determination to find him a Greek wife failed to sit well since it sounded like competition to my jealous mind and already covetous heart.

I had no way of knowing that sniveling and coughing next to him was his ideal candidate for a permanent liaison, albeit one with a red nose. Nor did I know he thought me adorable in spite of it.

Some perverse part of me demanded that I not allow him to see how attractive he appeared to me; after all, he was my employer and I'd already gotten burned on that sort of thing. Acting as professional as I could while sneezing, hacking, and sniveling, the impression I tried for was that I was appreciative of his role as my employer, but that I was less than taken with him which was a bald-faced lie.

What I didn't know was that Christopher Papadis was unaccustomed to that kind of response from women—even sick ones like me. My cool attitude sweetened the chase for him.

*****

Christopher was silent for a good while, focusing on the icy road with its deceptive patches of black ice. He couldn't help but think about the woman sitting next to him and her lack of response. Not that he expected her to fall into his arms, but the woman should have at least been grateful for the attention and help he gave her. Instead, she was merely courteous in her thanks and appreciation for his kindness.

Then on second thought, he realized he shouldn't have been surprised by her actions or lack thereof. After all, this was the woman who had eluded him at the Cloudland Community Center, leaving instead of a glass slipper, a fleeting memory he couldn't erase.

Marianna Ross was a tall, elegant woman, but there was more to her, something he appreciated instinctively—an aura of subtle intelligence and kindness. He watched as she held one-month-old Sarah Elizabeth Poteet close to her chest, nuzzling the little girl's head. It was enough to drive him mad with desire; he longed to see his child at her breast. He wanted to protect her and make her well again. Christopher Papadis was falling in love.

Be that as it may, the object of his adoration was sick now and needed him. That she was normally quite healthy and very independent, as demonstrated by her willingness to tough it out alone on the mountain, appealed to him tremendously, as did her attitude towards wolves howling in the night, encounters with bears, cougar tracks, and strange men. Nothing she encountered during her sojourn in the wilderness put her off her stride. This made him curious as to what kind of woman she really was. He wanted to know more.

*****

Listening to his silence and with no idea what he was thinking behind those dark, hooded eyes, I mentally assumed my reporter's disguise. Safely cloaked, I interrogated Christopher Papadis without appearing self-conscious, which I most certainly was underneath that sniveling, coughing exterior.

In a very short time, I knew that not only was "Lord Papadis" my landlord's business name, it was an authentic title. His large extended family owned olive groves in Greece and produced some of the world's finest olive oil under that brand name.

Titles and wealth impressed me very little, but since this man's riches enabled me to spend the past several months doing what I wanted, I felt a sense of obligation to him that was compounding rapidly. Illness gave me a surly edge, so I resisted his kindness, wanting to lessen the feeling of debt threatening to overwhelm me. I knew I looked awful, and I hated being needy so I tried for neutral. That wasn't easy to do considering the animal magnetism he emitted without apparently trying.

*****

It was after five when he and Rambo came by for me up at the clinic. I dreaded the ride back up the mountain in the dark and going back to my lonely retreat.

We dropped the prescriptions off at a ubiquitous corner drugstore and then found a small restaurant downtown for dinner while Rambo snuggled under the thick emergency blanket Christopher kept in the truck.

Before we left for home, we stopped to pick up the prescriptions, and I took the first dose to try and chase the illness away.

By the time we got back to the cabin, it was pitch dark. I was groggy again and sleepy and wanted nothing more than my bed. Correction: I wanted a good deal more, but I was too sick to let it happen just yet.

Clearly solicitous, and on a first-name basis by that time, Christopher saw me into the house, rebuilt the fire, and then brought more firewood inside before turning to leave.

Stifling a yawn that turned into a hacking cough, I gathered up my courage saying, "You've been so kind, but what I need right now is my bed."

Suddenly, he was overly solicitous of my well-being and even tried to help me to the bedroom. This I forestalled by reminding him of his promise to take the dog out before he left. Relieved when they left the cabin, I staggered into the bathroom, ran a comb through my hair, and gargled with mouthwash. Nothing, however, could help the dark circles under my reddened eyes or make my bulbous nose look remotely normal. Had I been fully sentient and looked out the window instead of into the mirror, I might have seen a different Christopher in the moonlight.

*****

Outside in the brisk cold of early night, Papadis pushed through the snow with Rambo under the shimmering silver light. He knew that he couldn't stay out long, as his body was already responding to the snow, dark trees, and full silver moon. When the big she-wolf appeared in the distance and howled for Rambo, he felt his own response rumbling in his chest. The dog sensed something but kept to his side almost touching his leg. It was time to take Rambo inside and then get away from Marianna before it was too late. She needed to know him far better before seeing what he really was.

*****

When Christopher and Rambo returned, my dog was full of himself. Shaking his entire body, he splashed snow everywhere, but he was so funny I had to laugh. For a moment, I forgot my assumed reserve as we toweled the dog and dried the floor. When we stood, Christopher was near enough that I could feel his breath on my hair. I sensed something different emanating from him in the blue-fire of his dark eyes and the way he held himself. I wanted to step back from him, but I couldn't convince my body to move away.

With his archaic manners and language, and now this, was he from a different time and place?

From the way he looked at me, I could swear that in spite of my runny nose and bedraggled looks, Christopher Papadis wanted me stripped naked and in the bed, sick or not. Instead, I took control and slid back from him, demurely offering my hand instead of the body and soul I dearly wanted to share.

"Thank you for everything, Mr. Papadis," I told him in my most formal tone. He took my hand in both of his and without thinking, I looked up and added, "Hopefully I won't be sick the next time you see me. And thank you for choosing me as the recipient of the residency grant."

Instead of releasing my proffered hand, he held it up to his perfectly shaped lips and kissed it. "Won't you please call me Christopher," he murmured, his lips hovering over-long in one spot near the middle finger.

At his probing kiss of that one simple spot, my knees almost buckled and my temperature probably elevated several degrees. Noting the deep fire in his dark eyes, I retrieved my reluctant hand, grabbed Rambo's collar, and nodded.

Speaking entirely too fast, I said, "Yes, and you may call me either Marianna or Mari. Thanks for giving Rambo a run, too. He was going stir-crazy in here with me."

Changing the topic of our conversation I told him, "I should have a draft outline of my paper ready for review later this week if you want to see it," and walked with him to the door. "I hope you'll attend my presentation before I leave if the weather allows."

"I would be honored," he said, bowing slightly from the waist before turning to leave.

Holding the door open just a crack, I watched him tramp through the snow, climb into the big truck, and drive away. He knew I was there because he slowed, let the window down, and waved just before disappearing from sight at the switchback. To this day, I will swear on every Holy book anybody ever wrote that he had a wolfish grin on his face. In the distance, silver, white, charcoal, and black shapes bayed at the moon.

The cabin felt empty without him in it. Pulling my grandmother's afghan off the mama-bear chair, I settled into the warm leather of the big one. Still imprinted with Christopher Papadis's body and musky scent, I let it caress me until I sneezed.

When I awoke around two a.m., it was to my dog howling and staring out at the window at another wolf howling in the distance. The drugs I got that afternoon must have been powerful indeed—had they kept it up all this time?

The fire had died down and the room was chilly. Nevertheless, I was quite warm, having dreamed about a tall man with dark skin and savage, fiery eyes. Reviewing the dream under cover of darkness, I saw myself standing in the door, watching him leave. Sensing my distraction, Rambo slid out and took off after the wolf pack that quickly hid him from sight. Completely ignoring my panicked calls, he disappeared in the blanket of white snow as the moon rose on the horizon.

Awakened during the night, I ran to the door just as Christopher Papadis stepped up to the porch. With my dog happily running behind him, he took me in his arms and kissed me. The taste and feel of him

73

were almost palpable in the dark. In spite of all my best intentions, I said, look, the road is slippery with ice. Stay.

Coming to myself again, I found the dream disturbing. Padding into the living room to banked the fire, I pulled Rambo away from the window and went to bed shivering, though not entirely from the cold. Even though Rambo snuggled up for additional warmth, sleep eluded me; I couldn't stop wishing the dream had been true.

Chapter 6

As my time on the mountain came to an end, the weather cleared and warmed up once more. Feeling human again, I went down to the Center the next Friday night hoping to see Christopher, but according to Nell, he was out of the country again. Deflated that he'd not told me himself, I let down my guard and decided to have a good time without him. I felt young and carefree dancing with the old geezers. I flirted with some of the younger men and gossiped with the women. After all, what did I have to worry about?

Fortunately, I had finally recovered from the congestion that nearly finished me off, so Rambo and I again hit the trails. The woods dried out and walks, while chilly, were again a pleasure. It was different, though. Instead of dry leaves with autumn's colorful beauty, nature's less vibrant colors intensified. Trees downed from the recent snowfall were dark against verdant ground mosses. Waterfalls raced off cliffs to crash below. For a short while, wildlife was more visible, too. I had never seen it so and rejoiced in being a part of it. Returning to hot, muggy Florida no longer held appeal; I wanted to stay on the Roan.

With the project nearly finished and my tenure at the cabin ending soon, I grieved over my imminent departure. I did not want to leave—not ever. Something in me said grab this beauty while you can. I made plans for a day hike on the Appalachian Trail the next day.

Taking advantage of good hiking weather, Rambo and I left in the chill just after sunrise. Using a barely accessible track near the cabin we'd found some time ago, I planned to trek to the marker and then spend the day on the AT. Rambo seemed unusually anxious to get to the trail, going so far as to pull at the short leash I allowed him. I had learned not long after he came to me that to give Rambo his head was to lose necessary control, but this felt different.

Sensing his urgency, I gave him that freedom and followed, guardedly letting him lead me for a change.

We'd been out several hours when we emerged from a stand of gnarled Rhododendron trunks. Rambo laid his ears back, tucked his tail down, and growled when we approached a shallow pit filled with dense scrub.

The hair on my head literally spiked at the roots when I saw what had his attention: a small booted foot protruded at an odd angle, not fifty feet from where we stood. I wanted to scream but nothing came out of my mouth. Nervous, I fingered the handgun in my pocket, pulling my dog, who resisted mightily, close to my side.

Knowing that what we were going to see was probably horrific, the tiny hairs on my neck began to tingle. "Oh, God, no, Rambo," I whispered. "What have you found?"

The fur on his back stood rigidly, his tail tucked under, confirming my worst fears as we made the approach. For a moment, I wanted to run away, but that I could not do. The rule of the trail is to help fellow hikers, not leave them helpless and alone in the wilderness.

It was far too late for the woman I found lying in caked blood. It looked as though she were dumped into the pit without ceremony. Stripped naked with her head back at an odd angle and legs askew, was a hiker, her backpack was thrown unceremoniously aside, her cap hanging on a branch.

Turning away, vomit spewed from my mouth in response to the fear I felt in my gut. Silent vultures circled high above; they had already found the body but had yet to land. Fortunately, they stayed aloft, no doubt begrudging our interference in their death ritual.

The forest was silent. Soft green moss at our feet and dense evergreen foliage above muted sounds on the great mountain. Frozen to the spot by the horror of what we had just found, I was completely unprepared for the voice calling me from nearby.

"Marianna, there you are!" I knew that voice. It belonged to Christopher Papadis, but there was a surreal quality to it. Surely not. Wasn't he supposed to be out of the country?

Sure of himself, he came striding into the clearing following our trail, tall, healthy, and of a piece. His approach upset two of the vultures, that sensing my distraction had landed on a low-lying branch. Obviously, they were anxious to begin their service to the dead.

Startled to see the vultures so close, he stopped and stared into the sky and then turned back to me, puzzled. "What is it, Mari? What have you found?"

Leaving the body behind, I staggered down the uneven slope to meet him with Rambo almost pulling me at the end of the leash. I thanked the gods for sending Christopher Papadis to me at that moment and fell into his arms sobbing with relief.

Rambo ran around, the two of us barking, cementing our embrace with his lead until Christopher exclaimed, "Whoa there, take your time you two, there's no hurry, is there? I went to the cabin to get your final report, found you gone, saw your trail note, and then followed you up here. I hope you don't mind the company."

"Mind his company," he had said. My God, I've never been so glad to see anybody in all my life! Off my game and unable to speak coherently, I failed to adequately express my relief at seeing him. Disentangled from the leash, Christopher roughhoused with Rambo without seeming to notice my reserve or my tear-stained face. When I failed to join in the play, he finally looked up and saw that all was not well with me.

He stopped suddenly to ask, "Say, why are you crying? Are you okay?" Then he realized Rambo was really pulling hard, trying to get him to follow. "Marianna, what's wrong here?"

At his words, an unnatural calm settled over me like a thick blanket. I stared up at the vultures again circling in the sky, and then back at him without speaking. Hot tears streaming down my cold face, I pointed to the shallow indentation in the earth's surface. "There's a body over there—a woman. Rambo practically dragged me up here instead of going on to the trailhead like I planned. From the vultures, I'm pretty sure she's dead but not long. How he knew is beyond me."

"No, I can't believe it! This is one of the safest places in the world," he said in a strained voice, staring again at the black scavengers peering down at us. "Do you want to show me?" The look of horror on my face answered that question.

I dropped to the ground to wait with my arms wrapped around Rambo, rocking, just rocking back and forth as Christopher followed the rough trail we'd made earlier. Knowing what he would find, it took all I could do to watch as he walked up to the body. It was as though he knelt in prayer for a moment, but then he looked up at the sky and rose to come back down to where we waited.

I finally had myself well under control. Ignoring my reserve, Christopher dropped to the ground and took me in his arms without saying a word. I wasn't sure who was comforting who, but I clung to him as though my life depended on it. When he finally broke the silence, his voice was roughened by emotion.

"Listen, I hate to ask this of you, especially since you've been up here too long already, but can you stay with the body until I can get down to my truck and call for help? Those vultures won't wait if we leave her alone. Twilight approaches, so I'll have to hurry."

In spite of myself and the grim situation we were in, I marveled at the old-world sophistication of his language. It was so beautiful and yet archaic.

Unaware of my foolish reaction to the anxiety of the moment, and taking my consent for granted, Christopher turned to leave but not before asking, "Have you a gun on you? If not, I will leave mine." Again he paused, intense concern on his face. "Perhaps you should come with me anyway."

I felt my stomach lurch with that queasy feeling again, but I showed him the small Glock handgun I carried with outward calm. The shooting range was one thing—I was technically prepared to protect myself— guarding a corpse in an isolated spot on a mountainside was a totally different scenario. The quiver in my voice betrayed me when I responded.

"Somebody murdered this woman, Christopher. No matter who she was or what she may have done, I can't leave her to suffer that final indignity."

Something on his face akin to respect let me know he approved of my decision. While I appreciated the sentiment, the choice to stay was mine.

"Nothing about this is good. We run risks whatever we choose to do. I must go; darkness is growing deeper," he said, his dark eyes glittering eerily. "Please keep your gun drawn and stay on alert. You could move up to the shelter and wait from there, but I think you need to be close enough to scare off the carrion eaters. Above all, try not to let Rambo leave your side. I will hurry. Shoot if necessary."

With that dubious reassurance, he took off almost loping across the uneven ground leaving me to wonder at the ease with which he moved in near-dark conditions. How could he possibly see his way downhill through dense foliage and over stony terrain like that? When a cougar cried out, it's voice uncannily human, I forgot any concerns I had for Christopher and hunkered down to wait, one arm around Rambo, gun in the other.

Rambo whined off and on while we stood watch. No sooner had Christopher disappeared from sight than the growing flock of anxious carrion-eaters dropped down a few limbs, gathering closer. One, especially, seemed intent on teasing me, hopping out to the edge of a slender limb. When the limb swayed under its weight, the big blue-black bird jerked, losing its grip and fluttered down towards the pit. Ignoring the chill and the loud beating of my heart, I threw a rock held at the ready at the great bird. At one time, it might have been amusing to see the flock swoop into the air at that, but I failed to see the humor in it.

Towards nightfall, a wolf howled in the distance. When my dog responded in kind, the hair raised on the back of my head and the eerie goose bumps I had come to know too well collided, chasing one another up and down my spine.

79

We kept our vigil well into the night, huddled close together, me and my dog. It seemed as though every rock that tumbled, every dead leaf that fell and every twig that broke reverberated all over the mountain while we waited. Bold, golden eyes glinted in the deepening darkness; an owl flew low overhead, hooting when it landed nearby. I swore I could hear footsteps in the crunchy leaves. A hungry cougar, tracking the scent of blood…, a black bear foraging…, or the wolves coming to take Rambo away from me? I thought the killer had surely moved on, but what if he/she had not. Two dead bodies instead of one would make headline news.

When Christopher returned bearing warm clothes, food, and water, I was astonished that even with good night vision, a headlamp, and a flashlight, he could find us under those pitch-black skies. Together we huddled close with Rambo between us to wait for the emergency mountain rescue squad, saying little. They seemed to take forever, and as a result, night sounds grew even more amplified as we stood by, guarding the body against predators.

Feeling like a frozen corpse myself, relief flooded every pore in my body when rumbles of the rescue squad's ATVs finally reached us. A strange glow lit up the woods when they roared up the mountain. Christopher set off a flare, and soon two all-terrain vehicles approached over the uneven ground.

We were relieved to see them but the men were all business. Imposing in their rescue gear they took charge of the situation. Ice-cold breath streaming out of my mouth with every word, I gave them a quick rundown of how Rambo and I had found the body. Christopher detailed how he had tracked us down and then went back to my place to call for help and for heavier jackets and flashlights while Rambo and I waited by the body.

Stamping around to keep the circulation moving, I think I chattered over much due to fear and cold, but when we led them over to where the body lay waiting, all sense of panic fled in the cold, hard light of death.

The corpse lay just as she had when we first discovered her, but now the bruised and naked skin held a sickly bluish hue under the piercing emergency lights, the notion of privacy null. Flies buzzed around the body, unheeding of the cold or the impropriety of their intrusion. It was just a day's work for the insects, but to me, their invasive labor was almost more heinous than that of the vultures.

The team beamed lights on the scene and set to work, stringing yellow police tape around the perimeter. One surveyed the area for evidence, while the other methodically checked the body in the harsh light, taking photographs from every angle. When they were finished, I was relieved to see the poor woman's body covered. Every nook and cranny of the illuminated area surveyed and assessed as much as could be under the circumstances, the battered victim was carefully zipped into a black body bag. They removed every torn scrap of fabric, her backpack, and cap, the walking stick, everything except for the one hiking boot that was missing when Rambo and I found her. That they could not find.

I wanted to ask, "Who was she? Where was she from? How did she die?" All of those questions died on my lips, unanswered. The rangers weren't giving information, they were collecting it, their faces cold, hard, and impassive under the beams of their ATVs and lanterns.

Instead, a prayer for the life that was lost came to me. Even that brief homage to the dead was rudely interrupted when they loaded the body onto a sturdy wheeled carrier attached to one of the ATVs. Then they turned to Christopher and me, firing questions like blazing bullets at the two of us.

Finally, Christopher interrupted saying, "Officers, this woman has been here for hours in the cold. Not only did she find the body, but she stood by while I went down to make the call for help. Surely the rest of your questions can be made in the warmth of the station hall and not out here."

One of the squad members mumbled, "Damned foreigner thinks he knows everything," under his breath. The squad leader heard it and quelled the man with a stern look. He then told us to get in the lead vehicle with him. When the ATV snarled to life with wired energy, Rambo fought getting into the wild beast of a vehicle, submitting only when Christopher and I pinioned him on both sides with our bodies. Not two minutes later when a wolf howled nearby and my dog responded, I questioned what that wild canine was really telling my dog, and how much the watcher knew. At any rate, Rambo settled down after that, and we took off down the mountain.

Had it not been in the wee hours of the morning, had there not been that body traveling behind us, and had I not been freezing, the windy zig-zag ride down the mountain might have been fun. As it was, that trip is firmly planted in my memory as one of the worst things I've ever experienced.

Finally assured the ATV wasn't a ravening wild creature come to kill and devour, Rambo enjoyed the ride, keeping his eyes and mouth wide open to the harsh wind. I, however, could not silence my thoughts. The gruesome scene replayed through my brain as we plummeted down the mountain. How did that woman find her way into such tangled undergrowth? Was she already dead when she got there or was she killed on site? And finally, where was the missing boot?

With a sudden jolt, I remembered where I'd seen the woman's face before—she was part of the Appalachian Trail maintenance group; she danced with Christopher Papadis the first night I saw him. He knew her! Why hadn't he acknowledged it when he saw her lying there in her own cold blood? His omission worried me. We were halfway down the mountain when I finally got myself under control and dared to look at him under lowered lashes. Christopher was pale as I knew myself to be, but there was also a closed, alien look about him.

Our teeth rattled as we flew over dark, rough ground, and my heart felt leaden, weighted down as with iron. I wanted to cry but refused to give in to the emotion. Instead, I buried my face in Rambo's snowy white fur and held on for dear life. He seemed to understand, tolerating my need for comfort without protest.

We flew through the woods at what seemed like an improbably high rate of speed. Finally accessing a service road, the ride went much smoother but it did little to soothe my agitated emotions.

*****

At the ranger station, we downloaded everything we'd seen and heard but the terse treatment we received felt more like an interrogation.

The same men who had been so kind at my arrival on their mountain three months earlier were cold and hard—all business. They wanted the facts about what we found, offering nothing in return but the woman's name, Stella Lewis.

Deposited back at the cabin just after dawn, we staggered in, turned up the thermostat, and lit a fire. Leaving Christopher to make coffee, I changed into fresh thermals, cords, a heavy flannel shirt, and a wool sweater. When I was finished, he took some spares from the carryall in his truck and changed as well. The much-needed coffee ready, I poured hot liquid into the dark blue cups, adding a dash of fine bourbon from my reserve stock to the mix.

Our experience on the mountain changed the dynamic between Christopher and me in ways that I could never have foreseen. I could not implicate the man with whom I was rapidly falling in love even when he grew distant and unresponsive. I surmised that it was up to me to get to the root of his actions and allow him to tell me the truth about him and Stella and why he had not identified her at the scene either to me or to the squad. Collapsing into my mama-bear chair to inhale the hot, steaming coffee, I pondered the grilling we endured that night and what I had to do now.

"During our questioning at the station, we were treated like suspects, not just the people who happened to find a body in an isolated place. If we were the perpetrators," I asked, "do they seriously think we would have called for help, stayed up there to protect the body, and endured freezing cold on a dark night if we'd committed the crime?"

From his tacit agreement, I gathered Christopher's questioning was definitely done in an accusatory manner. When he finally opened up, it was to say, "Jepson Kincaid, the one who called me a foreigner, treated me like I was a terrorist, accused me of it, actually," he said in sudden anger. "I don't know what his problem is, and I don't care, but being treated like that is unacceptable. I'm almost as much a part of this community as he is. I just don't have the bloodline he does."

Drinking his coffee in silence, he suddenly set the mug down and rose to leave. Seeing the hard set of his jaw and the cloud of worry on his dark brow I stopped him saying, "Christopher, don't leave. Let's make some breakfast first, okay? You're exhausted and honestly, I don't want to be alone right now."

It wasn't hard to convince him to stay, but at first our conversation was stilted, and I had to work hard to keep it going. He looked fatigued beyond endurance, as was I, but he was also hungry, and that was the key I needed.

Together we fried some bacon and then made grits and scrambled eggs. To make breakfast seem even more substantial, we made toast over the open fire. We ate in virtual silence sitting in our preferred chairs by the fire's comforting warmth. I waited patiently for Christopher to speak. I needed him to tell me what I wanted to know without my having to ask.

"Her name was Stella, the same woman who prevented our dance at the Center. She was a member of my trail maintenance team and for a very brief time, we were a couple. It was bad enough that you had to find her body up there, but for it to be someone I was once close to seemed impossible.

"I was so shocked that at first, I couldn't believe it was her. Wanted it not to be, but finally had to accept it." He paused then and dropped his head into his hands. When he continued, his eyes glittered with unshed tears. "She was a nuisance, was our Stella, and everybody on our team wanted to be done with her, but not enough to kill her. I don't know what to think, and I sure as hell don't know what to do or what to say about it."

His explanation helped, but it still didn't tell me why he failed to acknowledge knowing Stella at the scene. It was also bizarre that he showed up when he did.

"You know that I spent the last four years as a reporter, don't you?" When he acknowledged this, I continued. "One of the first things I learned to do when researching a story was to look at all of the angles without making a judgment. Who might have been irritated enough to get rid of her? Any members of the maintenance team, or somebody with something to protect? Is there anything more about you and Stella? Think long and hard because there may be a clue for us in the telling," I said, leaning forward in my chair. "When I saw you two dancing it looked to me like she was performing a mating ritual for all to see. She couldn't keep her hands off you in case you failed to notice. Was that for you or was she telling the other females to stay away from her man?"

Deep in thought, he stared into the fire before answering. His eyes, when he looked up, were almost black from grief and shock.

Ah, there's a lot more to this story, I thought to myself. When without a word, he held his hand out to me, I took it and let him draw me close. I settled into the big chair next to him like a mother hen with her chick. There was nothing sexual about it—just two people taking comfort from one another. Rambo looked up just long enough to make sure I was all right and then settled back with a grunt, his head draped over Christopher's feet.

"It wasn't the first time she acted out like that in public, and trust me, I found it acutely embarrassing," he said, resuming our conversation. "She's been doing it ever since she first laid eyes on me. For a while, she was successful because it was terribly flattering. By the time I realized what kind of person she was—clingy and demanding—I was basically labeled as her property. I don't like labels nor do I like people making presumptions about me."

"Just like Jepson Kincaid did during your questioning?" I said. "From what I heard through the walls, he accused you of luring Stella up there, killing her, and then going down to my place to create an alibi. From there, you supposedly followed my trail and 'found' Rambo and me with the body and then went for help."

"My God, you heard all of that through the walls? He's probably telling everyone I killed her," he told me ruefully. "Well, I can't alter the truth. My actions will have to suffice since Stella can't tell us who killed her."

Discussing what we saw and heard during our ordeal at the ranger station, patterns emerged for both of us. Questioned separately, I thought my treatment unnecessarily brusque, but what Christopher endured in the room next to me was primitive. Questioned by Kincaid, who called him an outsider and worse, a terrorist, he was cursed and yelled at until he feared assault. All of this, if his story was as he said, because he was a warm-skinned, American-born Greek who was in the wrong place at the wrong time. At that moment, apparently for his interrogator at least, he was an outsider, and probably the murderer of an innocent young woman. I was implicated as his accomplice, a role I never dreamed would be mine.

Repeatedly we played back what we had seen and heard, but the answers eluded us. My maternal heart wanted very much to give Christopher comfort but his voice was hard and cold as he recalled the treatment he received. Finally, he told me more about his relationship with Stella Lewis.

"Like I said, we had an affair. It lasted no more than a couple of weeks before I broke it off, but Stella was not one to give up easily. She started calling me almost every day, sometimes twice. She hung out at the Cloudland Center pestering Nell and the others to find out when I'd be there.

"Stella was stalking me the night you came. She knew I wanted to dance with you because she watched every move I made," he told me. "And she knew from experience exactly how to waylay me. She saw when you caught my eye, so she moved to sit behind you. When I stupidly signaled you from the dancefloor, she jumped before you could possibly make a move. What was I supposed to do—refuse her and make a scene? Things might have turned out differently had I gone over and asked you. Now she's dead, and you and I are suspects. It's like she's still after me."

So, he tried to dissuade her affections. He wanted her gone but not dead.

"She joined my hiking club shortly after we broke up," he continued, "still trying to get to me. Stella was high maintenance, so she needed help at every turn. But not from just anybody; it had to be me. The others were more than happy to leave her in my care."

"So that's one of the reasons you questioned her presence in that isolated location?"

"Correct," he responded. "She would never have gone up there alone. She couldn't have dealt with the area where you found her. I know it for a fact."

Resolving the issue of Stella's death was going to be complex, the reporter dwelling inside of me thought, *There are far too many loose ends.* Then I questioned if perhaps the killer was after me, too, although I couldn't imagine why.

Before I could say anything, Christopher resumed his line of thought. It startled me because it was so close to mine.

"I'm certain she wasn't off trail alone. She could never have handled that rough terrain. What I want to know is why she was killed so near the cabin. To my knowledge, she'd never been off trail in that area and she couldn't do it alone. What if it was you they were after and something went wrong between them?"

He left an hour later, but not before warning me to stay inside with the gun loaded, locked, and in my pocket at all times. "I've got meetings in Asheville that must be attended to. Won't you come with me? My mother would welcome you at her house, I'm sure. In fact, I'd prefer you do so, but it's your decision to make."

I liked the notion of going down the mountain with him since, at that juncture, staying alone was unappealing, but I wasn't ready to meet the family. I thought about cutting my time short and flying home for a break, but I couldn't do it. There was so little time left to the residency that I wanted to savor every moment of the time I had left at the little cabin. Besides, there were still a few people I needed to interview, and there was no way I'd leave Christopher to face his accusers alone.

While it was obvious that he disapproved of my decision to stay behind, Christopher Papadis was not a man to force his will on a woman. Instead, he read my mind. "Please take care of yourself, Marianna, and take no unnecessary chances. I will understand if you choose to go home for a while or even terminate your residency. You are free to go without penalty of any kind, but it's my hope that you'll continue with the project."

"Thank you for the consideration, Christopher, but I'd prefer to push through to the end. The murder probably has nothing to do with me beyond finding the body, so I can't imagine why I should stop working."

He accepted my decision and with a worried look, left me to ponder the whereabouts of a vicious killer.

Watching Christopher's truck until the taillights disappeared, Rambo and I went inside to what felt like an empty cabin. Bereft of his presence it was airless and stuffy and more than a little lonely. I suddenly realized how foolish I was to let him go and for choosing to stay alone. What if the killer lingered behind? All I had to protect myself with was the Glock, pepper spray, and Rambo. I had a pretty good idea what Rambo could do, but I had yet to shoot anything more than a range target under controlled conditions and devoutly hoped to stay that way. As for using the pepper spray, I could only hope to get it right.

In all of the agitation surrounding Stella's death, I hadn't even thought about calling my mother who seemed light-years away from me. Seeing her name and number pop up on my phone prompted an immediate guilty conscience. With her acute telepathic senses, she had managed to detect that her cub was in trouble without any help from me. Dreading her wicked tongue, I answered.

"Marianna, you've been on my mind since yesterday. When I heard that you found a body on that mountain, it scared me half to death. It was on the evening news. You can't hide anything from the news nowadays, if you'll recall. Now tell me, what on earth happened? I want to hear everything. Spill it."

Almost clairvoyant, she could see beyond the defensive tactics I employed to deflect her probing. I was already aware that what I wanted to withhold would cause the worry line between her brows to deepen measurably. Trying not to rile her further, I flipped rapidly through my mental story cards for a suitable answer, but none came.

There was no way I could protect her from my recent history—well, perhaps some of it—nor could I hide the truth from her, so I finally spilled the whole thing. She listened without interruption, but when I was done, she let fly.

"Marianna Ross, do you mean to tell me there's a crazy man on the loose up there? And then you tell me that you are alone in an isolated cabin on the side of a mountain, just you and Rambo? What on earth are you thinking?" She paused for a fraction of a second before resuming her tirade. "And how could that odious man, Papagou... Papadodo..., leave you alone in that cabin with a killer prowling about? I'd like to give him a piece of my mind!"

"His name is Christopher Papadis, Mom. P A P A D I S."

"Don't treat me like a child, young woman. I am perfectly able to spell, you know. It isn't necessary to sound it out for me."

I wasn't so sure about that, but I had to agree she had a point. My thought process, compromised by the events of the last two days, was functioning at limited capacity. The cabin provided an illusion of security but that's all it was. Killers often return to the scene after the deed, and what if he/she wasn't finished? And so it was that for a time, I reluctantly listened to reason.

We discussed the possibility of accepting Christopher's offer once I was cleared to go home to Florida. That way I could stay with her until I got the oral histories transcribed and the book finished. By the time we were done, though, I knew it was necessary to keep to my original decision: I couldn't leave Roan Mountain until the mystery was solved, and I was certain Christopher was safe from recrimination.

"Mom, I can't go. I can't leave here for a lot of reasons, number one being that I am apparently a suspect." She blustered at that. "Add to that, I cannot leave this project unfinished. You know I'm a hands-on kind of researcher—it's the journalist in me. It's non-negotiable."

My mom didn't like any of this, but she knew me well enough not to keep arguing. She'd done what she could, now it was up to me to forge ahead.

"You're not fooling me, Marianna Ross," she said before we rang off. I could hear the smile in her voice when she added, "It's that man. The Greek. He sounds delicious. I look forward to meeting him. And, honey, please be careful. If you can, try to leave the murder investigation to the authorities."

We hung up without my confirming her suspicions about Christopher, but in my heart, I knew she was right. There was no way I would leave him to fight this battle alone, but she was also wrong. I found Stella in that pit, and I would help find her killer.

I had just hung up with my mom when Cassie called. I dreaded having to speak to my nosy friend, but I picked up anyway.

Without a 'hello' or anything, Cassie dove straight to the heart of the matter. "Oh, Mari, I just heard about the murder on that mountain. Was it close to your place?" she said in her most solicitous voice.

Without waiting for a response, she started shooting questions at me non-stop. "Aren't you scared to stay in that wilderness by yourself, now? Are you coming home where at least you'll be safe? You barely know how to hold that gun you bought, much less how to shoot it. Do you want me to come up there? Maybe I could help."

The fragile olive branch offered after the harangue came as a surprise; our conversation just prior to my departure from Tallahassee was most unpleasant, and I had not forgotten it. Now Cassie was offering to come up to East Tennessee to stay with me on the mountain, ostensibly as my protector. No way. It was inconceivable that I could tolerate her in this situation, or any other for that matter.

Firmly declining the offer, I said, "Thanks, Cassie, but I'll be fine. I need to finish the interviews, and I want to do the transcriptions before I leave. Besides, the weather isn't really good for a visit right now. You wouldn't like it."

I regretted those last words the minute they came out of my mouth. The self-sacrificing Cassie, enamored of the idea of coming to my rescue jumped in to say, "Oh, don't worry about me and bad weather, Mari. I can take it. I'm tougher than you, like old shoe leather. Besides that, I talked to your mother last night, and we're worried about you being up there all by yourself. If you'll recall, I told you before you left how dangerous it was and sure enough, it has proved to be so. You shouldn't be alone and defenseless in that isolated cabin, and you know it. I could bring your mom with me if you like."

What she didn't know was that I was not completely alone nor was I without some means to defend myself. I'd practiced regularly at the shooting range since my arrival on the Roan, not because I liked guns but precisely because I was alone in an isolated place. So no, I didn't feel like having nosy company from Florida. Especially not Cassie and certainly not my mother.

"No, thanks, Cassie. I really appreciate the offer but I'm fine. Really."

It was funny to hear Cassie's voice audibly fluttering through the airwaves at my answer. Of course, there was a backstory to my response, but it was far more complex than I was willing to share with her. Had I done so, it would have been broadcast over the mountain tops and ridges and all the way around the state of Florida before sunrise.

What I said to myself was this: my teeth are sunk deep in the mystery behind Stella's death; Christopher needs my help whether he knows it or not, and I would tolerate no outside interference from either Cassie or my mother. How's that for an old-fashioned feminine response to trouble? Stand by your man and all that. Christopher Papadis was clearly not my man, but I was decidedly open to the possibility.

Sleep was long in coming for both the dog and me that night. The wolves seemed to be on the warpath with continuous howls that penetrated the walls until sunrise.

Every sound from the outside reverberated inside the cabin to torture me and keep Rambo awake and restless. Agitated, he paced from the front door to the back from just after midnight until dawn responding to the wolf's call each time it sounded in the woods nearby. I swear it was as though they were having a private conversation. I became a nervous wreck overnight from the noise and the very real fear that my dog might abandon me if he got loose.

Feeling vulnerable again, my defenses cracked a little. That's when Cassie's voice came back to haunt me. What was I doing on Roan Mountain alone?

The next morning, stiff and irritated from lack of proper sleep and worry, I took Rambo to the quick walk-about on the deck at daybreak just to be safe. Then I made coffee, puttered around the cabin, and tried to concentrate on the transcriptions.

I couldn't do it for the question that haunted me: Why was the wolf so close to the cabin, and what kept it there through the night?

Rambo, frisky as a pup, tried to convince me he needed a short walk, trying his best to get me out the door, but I was still hesitant. I wanted to be outside and on the trail to finish the ramble we started yesterday, but our world changed when we found Stella. In daylight's clarity, I realized there were too many unknowns outside that front door.

When I finally took him out, scattered snowflakes light and lovely swirled around us. Then Rambo, his needs forgotten for the moment, came to a dead stop, nearly tripping me. Lying directly in front of us just beneath a fine layer of new snow were sharply defined paw prints. That gave me pause. The wolf was on the porch steps, not somewhere out in the woods.

An eerily profound presence of mind settled over me like a cloak as I stared at those paw prints. The reason for it revealed itself when I grabbed the iPhone to take some quick shots. Directly beneath those of the wolf were clear humanoid boot prints pressed deep into the icy layer under the powder.

The wolf's ghostly presence seemed less important, and almost comforting now. The boot prints? No.

Etched clearly in the soft mush and then refrozen when the temperature dropped, they were made from heavy wide boots. Were they Christopher's from the day before? That hardly seemed likely because it was snowing when he left. His prints were long gone before he got out to the main road. So no, these tracks were fresh, coming long after his departure.

Before they blurred with the rising sun, I measured the shoe size and was able to capture clear renderings of the boot stamp on the arch of the sole with the smartphone's nifty camera.

Once I was done, Rambo, obviously concerned with the intrusion, nosed the area until all of the signs were lost in a mashup of dirty snow. Neither of us was overly concerned with the wolf signs anymore. They at least belonged to the mountain.

Please don't ask me why I didn't call anybody.

*****

I took a thermos and a mug to the deck out back when the sun rose higher. Bundled in thermals, fleece, and a wool blanket I was tolerably comfortable.

92

Something about that overlook soothed me. The cabin, tucked into a small cove near the summit, sat in the higher altitudes where snow-covered majestic evergreens reigned supreme. Below in the gorge, some of the deciduous trees kept their colorful leaves. The contrast under blue skies was beautiful. Soothed by nature's stillness, I settled down to ponder the situation.

I was intimidated by the boot prints but still not enough to run away. While I couldn't be absolutely sure whose prints they were, I was fairly certain whose they were not. Someone in need of help and who knew the Chi Roe symbol would have banged on the door to rouse the occupant. My next question was this: did the wolves frighten the intruder away?

So here is my force-field diagnostic on what to do: If I stayed on the mountain, I might be in danger but I might also get ole' Saul to sit still long enough to recount his stories at his place in the woods. If I left, I might be safer, but it would be far more difficult to communicate with my resources on the mountain. With hard winter approaching, the probability of getting caught in a serious snowfall was real. I might not be able to leave at all unless somebody came up to dig me out. Of course, that could be fun if it happened to be a man named Christopher, but I didn't want to put him under that obligation. In the end, I made the decision to stay and put my snowshoes to work; thus, my fate was sealed.

Chapter 7

More things than the weather heated up the next week. With so much activity surrounding the murder on Roan Mountain—sessions with the Tennessee Bureau of Investigation (TBI), identification, background checks, interviews with the press, gossip, and a potential murderer/rapist on the loose—I forgot all about Thanksgiving.

The trail was closed to hikers for the winter by that time and TBI was staked out at the murder site combing the area for every shred of evidence. It seemed to me TBI had the situation well in hand. Since their arrival, even the rangers treated me differently. Of Jepson Kincaid, I heard little to nothing. With no proof, I refrained from mentioning my suspicions about him.

Late Wednesday afternoon found me surveying an inadequate pantry. None of it even vaguely resembled the traditional Thanksgiving feast that I craved. At that point, my choices were few, either stay alone and make do with what I had, go to one of the larger towns like Elizabethton or Johnson City in the hopes of finding a restaurant open, or celebrate the holiday with the Cloudland community.

I chose the latter. It was a no-brainer, really. I needed people I knew, and I wanted holiday food badly enough that I might have tried to hike through a blizzard to get it. And, my employer might be there.

The only thing I couldn't arrange was family. I wanted my mother. Hard as she was to pin down, she spelled the only security I really knew and trusted. It seemed all we had in this world was one another, but she was far away.

I called Mom at 10 a.m. Thanksgiving morning. She's never been an early riser unless it was by necessity; the holiday was not an exception. It was wonderful to hear her voice, but she was clearly distracted when she answered the phone.

"Happy Turkey Day, Mom," I said when she picked up. The sound of pots and pans clanging in the background immediately got my attention. My mother was not alone. After the usual remarks, we came to an unnatural pause. I filled it with, "So, what are you doing for Thanksgiving?"

When she responded, her voice held a certain faux brightness to it. "Oh, I've asked a friend over, dear. We're both alone and decided to share the holiday."

I could sense she was hiding something. Having been a reporter, very little escaped me, and I knew my mother well. With the skills of an interviewer on the tip of my honeyed tongue, I asked a few questions, backing her into a corner from which she could not escape. The prevarication dissipated, and she spilled it: there was a new man in her life.

"So, Mom," I asked, all sugary sweetness. "When were you going to tell me about him? It's not like you to hold back. You should know by now that all I want is your happiness."

She made no mention that I withheld the news about the breakup with Jason for over two weeks before telling her.

"I know I should have called you, Mari, but this time, it's different. We began dating not long after you left. Please understand, this is serious. I just want to keep it to myself for a while."

She'd kept it secret from me for almost three months, which was a first. Mom flitted from one man to another, but I was always the first to know. I met some of those men, critiqued a few, even evaded a couple of badass types who wanted to flirt behind her back. I held her hand when she crashed on occasion, but this was different.

95

When my own matronly instincts came into play, I said in all sincerity, "Be careful, Mom. Take it nice and slow until you're certain, okay?"

"Oh, I will, dear. He's very special," she said. Then using her own highly polished communication skills, she switched gears on me without ever telling me his name. "So, tell me, have they found the killer yet?"

"Not yet. It's only been a couple of days, you know."

"But Mari, you're alone up there. Are they watching out for you and Rambo? I can't sleep for worrying about it."

"Mom, I'm okay for now. I decided to stay on at the cabin because TBI is staked out in the area where I found Stella. It's not all that far away, and they cast a wide net. The residency provider is also keeping watch, and my Glock is primed and ready, so I should be safe. Besides, I have Rambo, remember? Don't worry about me."

She wasn't convinced but knowing me well, decided to leave it alone. She was far more concerned about my plans for Thanksgiving. "But Marianna, I still don't know, what are you doing for the holiday, staying home? Having people over? Please tell me you'll not spend the holiday by yourself."

"No, Mom, I've decided to celebrate with the folks at the Cloudland Community Center. You know, I told you about them. Each year folks without close family come together for the Thanksgiving feast so nobody has to eat alone."

"And will the handsome Greek magnate be there?" she asked coyly.

"Aw, Ma, he's no foreign magnate. He's a Greek-American businessman but yes, he's supposed to be there."

She paused pensively for a moment and then said, "Promise me if he asks you to dance this time you'll say yes."

"That I will. I wish you could meet him, and these people, Mom, and see this place. Then you'd understand why I don't want to leave it anytime soon."

"Well, darling, perhaps someday I will see it. Meantime, you went up there to write," she said, "but it appears you've found much more than words with which to occupy yourself. Please be careful and take care. Have a lovely day and be safe on your mountain. I love you."

"I love you, too, Mom. I miss you so much."

"And I miss you, Darling. Enjoy yourself." The sound in her voice told me that while she missed me, she was ready to be off and onto other things, but so was I. As soon as we rang off, I hit the ground running. I had just enough time to shower and get down to the Center in time for the feast.

An hour later I was wearing my favorite look. I visited the village stylist for a haircut and color the day before, which proved to be a success, so I felt really good about myself. Hoping to see Christopher, I dressed in a warm, mossy green turtleneck, my favorite tweed jacket, tight dress jeans, and heeled boots, and left Rambo to guard the cabin. Worry about events from the past several days receded when I drove the Subaru around the mountain, turkey with dressing and pumpkin pie for dessert on my mind.

There were still a few coral and orange leaves here and there, the air was crisp, the sky an impossible shade of blue. My spirits were high until I passed the ranger station. Not fifty feet away from the road stood the man who'd interrogated and mistreated Christopher, taking a smoke. His stare froze my heart mid-beat.

Suddenly, the memory of the body I found on the trail flashed across my mind. The joy of the day fled in its wake as everything I saw and felt three days earlier rode in the car with me. Smothering under its weight, I couldn't turn it off, nor could I escape. But neither would I turn back. I gunned the little car into action, taking those switchback turns and hairpin curves like a maddened racer. It wasn't smart, but I felt more in charge of my emotions by the time I saw the Cloudland Community Center sign in the distance.

When I reached the Center, instead of a sophisticated woman-of-the-world, I probably looked like I'd seen a will-o'-the-wisp. Entering the building with a heavy heart and leaden feet, I questioned whether anything would ever feel normal again with each step.

Nell Baskins, who stood by the entrance greeting people, smiling at my approach. Seeing the distressed look on my face, she laid her hand gently on my arm and asked, "Mari, what on earth has happened to you, girl? You look like you've seen a ghost."

I let her hug me and then hugged her right back. The contact with another human being felt good enough that it brought me back to my senses. Staying close, she led me into the dining hall. When we passed the mounted black bear, I mutely gave it a respectful greeting. In my rattled frame of mind, I could swear it responded with a nod.

"I'm sure you're plenty upset from finding poor Stella dead and everything, but we're all glad you've come to celebrate with us in spite of it. It's at times like this that we need to stay close. Besides, Christopher Papadis is here. I was worried that he might not make it back in time since he had to go over to Asheville late yesterday on business. He's been watching that door like a hawk, hoping you'd be coming. Did he call you?"

When I shook my head in the negative, she went on to say, "That man! I can't believe Christo is still shy around you. Maybe today'll take care of it. He told me to let you know he's saved a place for you. See, there he is, at the table by the piano." Then she leaned in with a conspiratorial twinkle in her eye. "Christo's a keeper, girl."

She caught me by surprise with the mention of his name. I looked in the direction she pointed and saw him across all of those tables filled with people. He looked up at the same time, and we locked eyes. Though our connection was immediate I hesitated to move towards him. Instead, I froze, staying by the door near Nell, uncertain.

Without losing track of my eyes, he left the table, strode down the aisle, greeting people right and left, and then headed straight to where I stood. This time I did not run away from him nor did he shy from me. Instead, my heart did a complete flip when he gave me a bear hug for all to see, and trust me, they were looking. Had I been the swooning type and living in a different era, I might have required smelling salts, but he held me so close I couldn't have fallen very far. He looked good, smelled delicious, and felt even better.

Stunned and breathless, I let him lead me to the place next to his, sat primly, and going through the motions said, "Yes, thank you, I'd like half-sweet, and half unsweet," to his offer of iced tea. I was so taken by the sight and feel of him, that I would have said yes to anything he asked, but tea would have to do for the moment.

I had just been introduced to my seatmates when the bald-headed Reverend George Breeden stood to ask the blessing. Short arms folded over an ample belly, the preacher rocked on booted feet when he prayed, reminding us of how lucky we were to live on Roan Mountain. Then he delivered a mini-sermon, speaking to the good Lord on our behalf. He finished with a request for guidance for Stella's murder investigators. When he reached that part, I experienced that weird, tingly psychic feeling at the back of my neck again.

A slight movement in the room caught my attention and without actually meaning too, I looked up. Heads all around me were politely bowed, but one was not. From it, jet black eyes stared straight into mine. It was my new nemesis, Jepson Kincaid.

The old chill humans reserve for danger again snaked its way up and crawled back down my spine. I knew him, of course, but what I saw now took the acquaintance to a different level. I knew him from the day of the murder on Roan Mountain. He was the squad member who all but accused Christopher of collusion. I passed by him at the ranger station earlier, and now he was staring at me with malevolence during the prayer. I decided on the spot that he was the murderer. Without knowing why, I was positive his boots matched the prints outside my cabin door.

We stared at one another for one frozen moment. Everything I saw and heard the day I found Stella flashed before my eyes. I believe he knew what I was thinking at that moment and relished the thought of making me fear him.

There was danger in the room. I knew where it was coming from but for some reason, I wasn't afraid. I wanted to see what kind of shoes he was wearing but never got a chance. The minister ended his blessing. We all said, "Amen," and then everyone sat down to dinner.

I turned to tell Christopher what I'd seen, but he was already involved in passing bowls and platters down the tables. Thinking I'd only make a scene if I brought attention to myself, I set about having a good time in spite of what I had just seen and felt. Surely I was safe from Kincaid in the midst of this group of people.

99

My neighbors went all out for their Thanksgiving feast, with the food tables groaning under the weight of turkey and dressing and fresh roasted root vegetables from the harvest, with pumpkin and sweet potato pies for dessert. Their generosity and the sounds of laughter and children's voices piping accompaniment soon drove all thought of Kincaid to the back of my mind.

The food was delicious. It was everything I hoped for down to giblet gravy drizzled over divine cornbread dressing. It's my hope that I didn't act like a pig that day, but the act of consuming that food was significant. I still missed my mom's Thanksgiving dinner, but Nell and her friends did an excellent job of standing in for her.

Christopher was solicitous of my every need, and I took what he offered with a glad heart. It seemed that during the feast, his chair drew closer, and when his leg found mine and remained close, touching from hip to ankle, I welcomed it.

When the turkeys were finally stripped to the bone and we were stuffed, I leaned back and sighed in contentment. His arm curved across the back of my chair just as if it had done so for years. I let it stay there.

I saw Nell exchange knowing glances with her interested neighbors as word continued to spread about Christopher and me. It was a living commentary that flew with the speed of light from one diner to another, a friendly message running in circles across and around the big tables. Awareness of the love from my temporary community broke something inside me. Tears welled, so I excused myself, leaving raised eyebrows in my wake.

The hallway was empty when I reached my friend, the mounted black bear. Standing next to the glass case sniveling, I took strange comfort from its benign presence. That's where Nell found me. A comforting grandmotherly figure, she took me to her capacious bosom and rocked me like a baby. That gesture unleashed a real flood of tears, but she held on, a bedrock in my time of need.

How, I wondered, in the midst of so much love and happiness, could I have found myself in such an awful situation? A wonderful man I wanted to love, a dead woman with whom he had a connection, a renegade ranger who probably came to my porch during the night, and whom I caught staring at me with vitriol. To top it all off, I was far from home. Yes, it was too much.

When the tears finally slowed to a sniffle, she handed me a crumpled napkin and said, "It's alright, Baby Girl, it's all right to cry. We love you on this here mountain, and we'll try to care for you if'n you'll let us. You've done some good work up here, and we really appreciate it. What you're goin' through is awful, but it's nothing you can't handle if you put your mind to it, and we're all behind you. Of one thing we can depend on: Christopher Papadis will make sure they catch the person who killed that woman and plant him beneath the prison for life."

"I know what you're trying to say," I stammered. "But you weren't there, and you didn't see her lying bent and twisted in that pit of overgrown weeds. I can't sleep for seeing her exposed to the cold and those vultures waiting to come down for their feast. Had Rambo and I not gone out that day—"

She interrupted me at that point to say, "But you did go; it was meant for you to find her." Her comment released yet another torrent of tears. "There, there, Sweetheart, it'll be all right. Nothing can hurt poor Stella now, and you are safe with us."

Now that my barriers were down, I had to get it all out. "I know all that, but you didn't hear what that ranger said about Christopher when they got to us, or how they treated him at the station. My questioning was bad enough, but I could hear what the ranger said to Christopher and it was much worse. That same man was here today, staring at me with what looked like pure hatred during the blessing!"

"Child do you mean to tell me you didn't keep your eyes closed?" This she said in a playful manner, but then Nell's expression turned serious. "I think I know who you're talkin' about. That was Jepson Kincaid, the newest member of the rescue squad. I was standin' by the door when he came in and saw his expression when he saw you were with Christo. I couldn't tell if it was jealousy or what, but it looked plenty bad to me. I can't imagine the captain, Ransom Russel, letting that boy question witnesses. He's a tracker, not an investigator, especially with him being so new to the job. I've known him since he was in diapers, and he's been trouble ever since he learned to walk. Seems to me he should have grown out of his bully'n ways by now, but maybe not. He knows this mountain better than most. That's why they hired him. We'll keep an eye on that one."

Somewhat mollified by our conversation but not completely, I turned away, only to be stopped by Nell's worn, plump hand on my arm. "Listen, Mari, I know this is not what you had in mind comin' up here and all, but you're not alone. It's a bad situation, what with Stella gettin' raped and then killed, but you were up there, and you did find her in that pit, and now it is part of your task to find the answers. Trust me when I tell you that somebody will pay for killing her, but it won't be you or Christo.

"As for Christo, that man is pure gold. He wouldn't hurt a flea unless it was bitin' somebody he cared about, and I'm telling God's own truth when I say it. We're kinda' particular about who we accept on this mountain, but there's never been a newcomer we took to like we have to him unless it's you, and it looks as though he likes you a lot."

Her comments helped alleviate my angst about finding Stella and the treatment we got after, but that last bit took me by surprise. "Is it that obvious? How can you tell?"

Nell laughed at that and said, "Well, if you can't see that his heart shows plain as day when he looks at you, we're all in trouble. Besides, we saw ya'll sittin' close as can be just now, and I first saw it that night he tried to catch you when you left so suddenly." When she saw the expression on my face she said, "You didn't know we were all watching the whole thing, did you, Cinderella? I was standin' next to Christo when you walked in, heard him catch his breath and stand to attention in that way he has. Instead of going over to ask you, he tried to get your attention for the dance, and that flirt Stella flitted in and took the dance from you.

"Then it was me that held his hand when you ran off. He stormed back in here like a thundercloud about to burst, saying he wanted to wring Stella's sorry neck for runnin' you off. And then I had to waylay her so she'd leave him alone the rest of the night. She was out to get him but mad as a hornet because he wasn't havin' anything to do with her. Some people never learn, and she was a prime example of that kind of person."

The picture she painted of Christopher Papadis that night was about as far from the way I saw him as one could imagine. In spite of myself, I giggled.

"So you think it's funny too, do you?" she said, a fierce look on her plain face. "Well, I'm here to tell you we've been trying to find a good woman for that man for years. When she first came along, we thought for sure it would work out but that's before we got to know her. It didn't take us long to figure out what she was after, but by that time she had her claws into him. Nobody knows for sure how he finally persuaded her to leave him alone, but she never got over him, as you could see that night."

"You know, come to think of it, I wonder if Stella was spying on you the day she got killed. I know she was a good enough hiker in spite of pretendin' to look helpless because I saw her on the trail one day. But don't nobody like to walk where you and Rambo found her with those thick brambles coverin' that pit. Turns out she was a foolish woman, and now she's gone. Oh, dear me, I shouldn't speak so of the dead, should I?"

Then she changed the subject so completely it took me off guard. "You feelin' better now, child? We need to get back in there because the fiddlers are tunin' up for dancin', and the ladies are about to serve the pumpkin pie."

She waddled away, swinging her hands to the beat of the music with me in tow. Just before we turned to reenter the hall, I glanced up at my old friend the black bear, and this time I could swear that he winked at me.

Entering the hall, I found myself swept onto the dance floor in the arms of Christopher Papadis. Folks danced around us, but I could swear on the Holy Book that they left a good amount of space for us to move around in by ourselves. My angst over Jepson Kincaid dissipated under his spell.

The first group was a blend of amateur musicians. What they lacked in expertise they made up with enthusiasm. Then about fifteen dulcimer students sat on the stage together and led by the emcee, happily plucked a few holiday tunes. The music moved up several notches when their exuberant teacher, the emcee, switched hats, kicked off her shoes, and got up on the stage to play the bass next to a tall, thin fiddler dressed in black. When he set the fiddle to his chest and began to play, she started dancing, twirling the bass in her hands. There was no question in my mind that we were in for a good time. I stayed for the whole thing.

Christopher maneuvered me the entire afternoon, and this time not even the ancient papaws dared ask for my hand. We danced together, listened to the music and, in general, got to know one another much better. When he offered to accompany me home, oddly enough, I refused the offer.

"You're not going to play Cinderella again, are you?" he asked, a small smile hovering on his sensual lips. Gazing into his dark eyes I pondered my obtuse refusal because the notion of inviting him to come home with me was appealing. But no, I wanted to replay every minute of my time with him that day in the silence of the woods. Above all things, I didn't want to rush into anything. If, and when, I invited him to come home with me, it would not be a casual affair.

And so it was that after a richly rewarding kiss that almost made me regret my decision, I reluctantly turned away and let my little Subaru scoot back up the mountain, getting back to the cabin just after nightfall. Instead of feeling welcoming, my retreat was dark.

Chapter 8

It was black as pitch when I pulled under the carport. I expected the light to come on. It did not.

Glad that I put my smartphone on the charger on the way home, I turned to the flashlight function to find my way to the porch. The motion detector should have flipped on. There was no sound from within. All was silent.

Beginning to feel panicked, I called out, "Rambo, are you in there?"

Hearing nothing in response—he always barked and scratched at the door—I panicked. What was going on? "Rambo! Where are you, boy?"

Then it occurred to me there was no resistance when I pushed the key into the lock. Instead, the heavy scarred door creaked open almost as if by magic.

Fear rode me then. Was someone inside the cabin waiting? Was it the one who killed Stella? Where was my dog? I had to know if he was hurt. Gathering up what little courage I had left, I pushed the door open.

Frantic now, I called Rambo but got no response. Thankful for the light on my phone I quickly surveyed the few nooks and crannies he could have crawled into if he were hurt, but it was a fruitless effort; I already knew Rambo was gone. Why had I stayed out so late? Why had I insisted on coming home alone? I felt stupid, fragile, vulnerable, and angry all at the same time.

That there had been an altercation there was no doubt. Papers and chair cushions littered the floor, but the damage to my grandmother's afghan was the worst part. It was a shredded mess, with the bulk of it in the ashes of the cold fireplace.

Calling Rambo's name over and over again in vain hope, I pulled the filthy pieces of knitted yarn into my arms, and then sat on the floor and folded in on myself. Teeth clenched, arms and legs crossed, my stomach roiling in bitter anger and frustration, I bawled like a baby.

Unbidden and certainly unwelcome, sanctimonious Cassie's voice came back to me loud and clear. I was a fool to have left the security of my home in Florida for this isolated wilderness filled with unknowns.

Afraid to leave, and even more, afraid to stay at the cabin, I called Nell and told her what happened. In less than an hour, I heard a truck's engine and saw the headlights snaking up the gravel track to stop at the base of the steps.

It was Christopher Papadis who stood framed in my door. Backlit by the truck's headlights, his stance like that of an angry God. At that moment, I would not have been surprised had Zeus struck amidst thunder and lightning.

"Why didn't you call me?" he demanded in a harsh voice without taking a breath. "Why did Nell have to tell me about this? Don't you trust me, Mari?"

I really didn't have a good answer other than I didn't want to seem helpless or dependent on the man. Besides, I knew Nell far better than I knew him at that point.

"Rambo is gone," I told him, shivering in shock. "And look at this. My grandmother knitted it for my high school graduation," I said nothing more, just sat in the dark in front of the cold fireplace holding the filthy pieces of my grandmother's handiwork, mourning the loss of my dog.

The hurt and anger Christopher directed at me shifted rapidly to horror and remorse when he realized my reaction was more than justified; the attacker's focus was now aimed squarely at me. I was now the target.

Seeing my sooty, tear-stained face and what I held in my arms he dropped to the floor with a curse and held me in silence until the shivering passed.

"Nell called the Sheriff and Ransom Russell at the ranger station, too, so they'll be up here soon," he said, clearing the big leather chair off and reassembling the cushions. "Let's stay put and wait in here until they come. They'll need to talk to you." Before I could agree, he scooped me up as though I were no bigger than a child, and settled me in his arms to wait, his chin resting on the top of my head.

A part of me wanted to bury itself in him and find forgetfulness, but I couldn't do it. Worry about Rambo and the implications of what had been done to my possessions consumed me.

We sat close together in the cabin's dim light speaking little. He dozed off eventually but I could not. Finally, I slid out from the warmth of his arm and rose to stoke the fire and boil some coffee. When I returned with steaming mugs of rich mountain-grown brew in hand, the haggard look on his face confirmed my suspicion—he, too, was worried.

Embarrassed to be caught napping, he thanked me, took the coffee in one hand, and then tried to straighten his clothes and hair with the other. I had just spent the night in his arms without so much as an erotic tingle, but now, at dawn, something about his actions was deliciously appealing.

Before I could turn away, I got a taste of what to expect if and when we did continue. He set the coffee down and stood to take me in his arms and without a word kissed me so deeply my toes curled from the heat. I felt aligned with him in a way that brooked no refusal. I belonged in those arms, and I wanted more.

From the look on his face and the hardness pressing against my belly, I was pretty sure Christopher felt the same way. He nuzzled my hair and speaking close to my ear said, "Not now. The law and the Mountaineers will be here any minute. We'd better be respectable when they arrive."

Reluctantly drawing away, I turned instead to the kitchen. Rummaging through the refrigerator I found enough eggs to scramble while Christopher made toast over the fire. We ate in companionable silence.

While we waited, I told him what Nell told me about Jepson Kincaid. About seeing him outside the ranger station on my way to the

Center, his late arrival to the Thanksgiving dinner, his hateful glare during the blessing, and his early departure.

"If you had seen that man's face when I looked up, you'd have thought he hated me," I told him. "He didn't even have the grace to stare through lowered lids. This was full on. The scary thing was that there was nothing I could do about it. When I told Nell, she warned me about Kincaid. Nell says that while I may not have heard his rattles, that look was just as dangerous. It was a warning.

"And when I called her last night, she said that when she packed him a to-go box from the diner, he supposedly left to go back up to the ranger station. He had plenty of time to break in here because I was gone the entire afternoon."

We covered a lot of distance in that dusky between time, the tenuous space between the dark of night but not yet daylight. His expression grew incredulous when I told him Nell saw Stella and Jepson together in the Elizabethton Ingles parking lot. Frankly, it was hard for me to believe too, but I trusted Nell and believed the story. "I kid you not, she said they were huddled close as anything in Stella's car in broad daylight," I told him, "but he either said or did something she didn't like, and Stella slapped him hard. He got out of the car and stalked over to his truck and growled out of there like a mad beast or something. Then Stella combed her hair, fixed her face, and strolled into the store like nothing happened."

"Surely Nell was mistaken. I can't imagine Stella with Jepson Kincaid," he said in disbelief. "Did it look like she deliberately tried to provoke him?"

"I have no idea. Remember, I only saw her alive the one time, and you know my thoughts about that. You'll have to get the details from Nell."

It was my turn to be astonished when Christopher shared what happened when Stella joined his hiking group and how her brazen flirtation backfired on her, big time.

According to him, they met in a bar in Johnson City. "She was attractive with an athletic build and very attentive, telling me she'd come to hike the Appalachian Trail. I gave her my card when I left and thought no more about it until she showed up at the Community Center. That led to our brief liaison, but after the first time, it was no good. She was clingy and manipulative. I won't tolerate that from anybody. I broke it off, so she found a sponsor for membership in my hiking club. One of the guys took the bait, but once she got in, Stella dropped him and went to work on me."

She soon alienated him from his friends by pretending to need help all the time and by refusing assistance from other members of the close-knit group. Soon, they left her to him and moved on, an unfortunate fact that failed to sit well with Christopher Papadis.

Considering where we found her, he had other questions. "There's hardly anybody on the trail right now. It's closed until late Spring. We've had no more major storms, so it should be relatively clear of debris. I can't imagine that one of the local club members would go up there with her," he said.

Staying well away from one another in our respective chairs and heavily aware that Rambo should have been on the floor between us, we batted ideas back and forth by the fire's light. By the time we were done, I knew with certainty that no matter how irritated he had been with her, it wasn't enough to do away with the delusional woman Stella Lewis had been.

With daybreak came more surprises. My laptop and all of my Roan Mountain research files were missing. Fortunately, I kept the lanyard with the flash drive with me, or all might have been lost.

What looked like smudges on the door frame the night before now showed rusty red. "Christopher, that's blood. It's on the door and there are pieces of torn clothing just outside on the porch and down the steps. Whoever broke in sustained damage, there's no doubt about that, but what about Rambo?"

Will the desecration never stop?

No sooner did that thought hit me than the rumbling sound of trucks intruded. We really hadn't waited as long as it seemed, but it felt like forever to me. Even though it was cold with dense snow clouds lowering overhead, we herded everyone around to the back deck so the sheriff's team could search for evidence inside the cabin. Soon there were at least fifteen people back there, stomping in a fluttery snow shower, blowing icy smoke, all talking at once.

"You'n's listen to me for a minute," said a contralto voice somewhere in the middle of the group. I knew it was Nell, even though I couldn't see her. While I was surprised to hear the authority in her voice, I was even more impressed to see those tough mountaineers listened to her. Would wonders never cease?

She held their attention with a stern authority that brooked to refusal, standing in their midst, all 4'11" of her. "The law has got the house covered, but we've got to find that white dog of Mari's if we can, and we've got to find which way the intruder went. While I'm not namin' names, we already have a good idea as to who that might be. Jack Holcomb's gone after Saul to bring him and his dogs to help us track our man."

I stared at the woman slack-jawed with amazement when she turned to me. "Marianna, would you care to ride with me?"

Knowing it would be in extremely poor taste to refuse her invitation, I grabbed my walking stick. All I really wanted was a hot toddy and my grandma's shredded afghan all of a piece, but it wouldn't be that day.

"Jake, you take Tuck and Hotdog and hit the AT up around the rest area closest to where they found Stella. John, you and Christo push deep into that holler where this girl found Stella. Ain't no crime ever been committed didn't the killer leave something more behind. Find it. The rest of you, wait for Mr. Saul and the dogs and then follow his lead. Me'n her's gonna find Rambo an' bring him home." Not one of us thought to question her.

Just then an old truck came rattling up the track bearing the legendary tracker and his merry band of barking beagles. He carefully slid out of the driver's side, signaling to the dogs who went quiet on a dime. "Who you want us to find, Ms. Nell?"

Quickly she briefed him on what was happening, to which he responded saying, "My take on it is this: that boy Jepson knows these mountains better'n almost anybody but me. I expect he's in a hidey place that'll be hard to find, and he won't come out of it unless we make him.

When he does, he'll be mad, and we'll have us a hornet's nest. But first, we gotta find him."

There was general consensus all around, with boots scuffing rocks underfoot and the occasional steaming spit of tobacco juice landing in the bushes. With them in agreement, he turned to Nell, "Split 'em up and spread 'em out. We'll meet back here later. You and that girl better get the dog—the sooner the better." Then he turned to me.

"Don't know as though that dog's gonna want to come back, especially not if'n he's gone off with his friends. My take on it is this: let that dog find you. If he wants to come back, he will. If not, you gotta let him go."

I agreed to the plan, but I had my doubts, too. Would Rambo voluntarily give up his freedom? I had no way of knowing, so I prepared myself for the worst. Looking out over the distant mountains, I knew a sense of foreboding. Dense knowing clouds hovered over the tops of those old misty mountains in layers of gray from oyster to pearl to bluish-charcoal.

I wanted to speak with Christopher before we left, but there was no time. The crew, all business now, split off on their assignments, loading up before I could get my act straight.

Nell, seeing my dazed look broke in to say, "Come on, Mari, an' bring that bamboo walking staff with you. Let's go find your dog." My father would have been proud had he seen how his daughter listened to authority that day. All business now, I thrust my angst aside and without protest, picked up the long staff, and followed her.

Climbing into Nell's cherry-red pickup, it felt as though I had gone back in time and this served as a distraction. My grandfather always drove a pickup, only his preference was for blue, plain metal Fords which were so high up that I needed a stool to reach the cab. Nell's, in contrast, was easy to climb into, nicely furnished, and clean as a pin, but it still gave off that no-nonsense aura that Granddaddy's truck did. I loved the way she drove slung back in the seat, left arm propped on the window, controlling the steering wheel with one finger, left leg crooked just a bit. This left her right hand free for gestures, something she did frequently.

Something about the whole thing rattled me. Had my grandfather been reincarnated into this sturdy woman's body? The Lord only knew, but I had a strong feeling about it.

At her signal, the small fleet of four-wheel-drive vehicles rolled out with Nell's red truck in the lead. Ransom Russel, the ranger captain who allowed Jepson Kincaid to question Christopher and me, was clearly at fault in their eyes and no longer trustworthy. As a result, their faith in him was severely compromised. Let him do his investigating. Meanwhile, the mountain folk would conduct their own.

These people were literally taking the law into their own hands, and now I was part of them and complicit. Frankly, had I been Kincaid encountering those mountaineers, I would have given in on the spot.

As though she could read my thoughts, Nell broke into my reverie saying, "We take care of our own on this mountain, girl. One of us goes wrong, we do what we have to. Don't tolerate nobody messin' with our people."

Getting the opportunity to ride with their leader couldn't have been better for me. For all that Nell was plain-looking and plain-spoken, I was drawn to it. There was a deep wisdom residing in her that was rock solid.

She navigated those mountain roads like a NASCAR driver, directing the search from various sites with cool authority.

The cool-headed mountain woman, wearing not a stitch of makeup, her white hair haphazardly clipped up on her head in a scraggly bun, commanded total allegiance with little to no effort. Having her all to myself, except for the reason for our journey, of course, was perfect.

No sooner had we gained the main road than my interviewer's hat dropped into place, and I was off and running in my role as a story collector. I'm quite sure she knew what I was doing, but she allowed me the opportunity with grace. Besides, it was her way of keeping me from turning into a worrywart. I think we both knew that.

As it turned out, Nell's people arrived on the mountain, which straddles both North Carolina and Tennessee, long before either became states. "There were Indians here then—Cherokee, and Creeks, mostly. Giant trees towered all over the place. Eventually, the settlers drove most of the First People away, pushing them ever westward, and they cut most of the big trees. I'm real sorry about all of that, but I love this place right here, right now, just the way it is. It's where I belong."

When the road got too rough for conversation, Nell stopped talking in order to focus. Lost in thoughts about my own presence on the mountain, I left her to it.

We entered places I didn't know existed, stirring undercurrents that had to do with ancient memories lying buried in its depths. It was almost as though we were transitioning from the real world to that of the primordial. In that isolation, trees grew taller, the environment a surreal fantasy.

*****

The searchers gathered back at my place for lunch and to discuss our options. By that time, they had isolated the general area of where Jepson was probably hiding and the wolf den as well, but there was more—the presence of an anomaly—tracks that were bear-like, but not quite, nor did they appear to be from wolves.

I thought of Rambo out there with an otherworldly shape-shifter stalking him. I had not bargained for such phenomena on this mountain and thought of all the times Rambo and I spent out there alone. Then I remembered his anxious pacing during the full moon just a few days prior.

At the time I just thought it was the wolves nearby that caused his angst. Now I wondered. Concerned that Nell would make fun of me, I told her about it, but instead, I got a nasty surprise.

"It's more than possible for some strange creature to be up here, Marianna. There have been rumors of sightings and a lot of talk about it. This place is ancient beyond memory, and these are the oldest mountains in the world, so why not? Maybe Stella stirred something up she couldn't handle. Maybe that's what got her kilt."

Had I not been looking directly at her, I might have passed out then and there, but Nell wasn't trying to be funny. She was speaking the truth as she understood it.

"There's a Jack Tale. You might call it applied storytelling under the circumstances that we like to tell up here. It probably came over from Europe with the settlers, but it's Appalachian now. Maybe it'll help you understand what we might be dealin' with better."

Without losing focus on the road, Nell began to tell the story in her pure mountain twang. I listened in silence, completely spellbound by the tale from the minute she opened her mouth.

"You see, there's stories called Jack Tales here in Appalachia. They're told all over the world, really, an' migration bein' what it is, most are related, but here, Jack is pretty special. We've had all kinds of collectors up here tryin' to get the stories down on paper. They ain't the same when they're stuck in a book, but sometimes those tales explain things we don't have answers to. I'm thinking we've got one of those.

"I read one that a professor from East Tennessee State University collected that sort of fits this situation. It's the one about when Jack leaves home to seek his fortune because he and his mama are gonna' starve if he doesn't. Now that part is common, but it's what comes next that's unusual. He finds out there's an evil spirit runnin' loose at night, terrorizin' everyone, murdering some, and robbing others of speech including a pretty girl in need of a rescue. She had such a bad fright as a little girl that it plumb robbed her of speech. He sets out to help her find that awful thing and when they do…"

When Nell paused the telling to focus on navigating off-road, I glanced at her. She was so deep in the tale that I could tell her driving was by rote instinct. It was the story that mattered at the moment. I was relieved when that rusty twang cranked up again so that I could hear the rest of her story.

"They say Jack and the girl defeated the evil spirit. The boy got hurt and that blue-eyed girl fought her own battle by staring back at it, straight in the eye to save him. That thing plumb disappeared into thin air. They say that girl never did stop talkin' after that. It must not have bothered Jack too much. They brought his mother to live with the girl's mama, then they built a cottage nearby and had a passel of children of their own. Of the evil spirit, they never heard another sound. Supposedly, it was gone for good, but what if it wasn't? Or maybe there's another one? There's almost always a root of truth in those tales.

We were silent a good while after that, thinking about the implications of the story in relation to what we were dealing with. Thank goodness Nell knew the terrain well because we crossed gullies and rough spots I would never have attempted. She parked the truck deep in the woods you'd never find unless you knew the area really well. Once on location, we set out to lure my dog using me as bait. As per the master-tracker Saul's instructions, Nell wore one of my jackets and carried Rambo's harness and leash so as not to totally confuse the scent. We walked about a quarter of a mile following the markers Saul had set out for us earlier. She constructed a makeshift blind nearby and then virtually disappeared.

At Saul's direction, I still had on the same clothing I wore the day before. This was to make my allure more pungent. After all, mine was a scent Rambo knew and understood, but I had little faith in this maneuver. I was well aware of the wild nature that underlay his amenable exterior. No way was Rambo going to walk out into the open and leave his new pack, but I was willing to try whatever it took to convince my dog to come back.

From my damp perch surrounded by a dense cloud, I called Rambo until I was hoarse. For all of my efforts, I got nothing more than chatter from a bunch of crows who found me a curiosity. A lone bald eagle watching from a spruce pine some distance away kept vigil.

At sundown came the sound we were waiting for—a wolf calling in the distance. The howl echoed closely, and then another started where it left off. I shivered at the primal call. Did one of those howls belong to Rambo? I could only hope so because I could not distinguish between them. With nothing to prevent sound from traveling it was obvious that they were drawing closer. Darkness settled around the ridge like a cloak. That had me worried, but at least the clouds were gone. Rambo, I would be glad to see, but not his new friends. When I finally saw the barest glimmers of white moving among the rocks and boulders, they were headed straight for me. Rambo?

In the lead was a magnificent wolf with the silvery deep ruff about its neck and sleek powerful muscles that moved with every step. Unafraid, the pack-leader paused at the edge of the tree line to stare at me with golden eyes.

Eventually, what must have been the whole pack gathered in a half-circle around him, waiting not far from where I was perched. Alone on the boulder's broad surface, I was profoundly grateful to know that Nell was hiding nearby with her rifle at the ready. The pack seemed not to notice or else they didn't care.

Again, their leader threw its head back and howled, followed by all the others. The sound was at once oddly harmonic, surreal, and incredibly powerful. When the howling ended, one of the animals passed through their ranks to stop at the foot of my rock. I said nothing. When he turned back to the pack, I felt his anxiety. He longed to stay in the wild with this pack. Something in me responded to that need and for a moment, I wanted him to remain free. Had we not needed his help to find Stella's killer, I might have just let him go wild. Instead, the all-too-vivid mental image of her naked body splayed out in the pit flashed before my eyes and I had to call him.

"Rambo, come."

He turned back to me, at first with seeming reluctance. With one tentative step after another, he moved up the pitted rock. When he stopped directly in front of me, it was of his own volition. With eyes downcast and hands in my pockets, I willed myself not to touch him but to wait. From what I could see, the past few days had not been without trauma. There were missing patches of fur, his coat was discolored, and a ragged scratch over one eye reminded me of when we first met. Still, I could feel his loyalty reaching out to me. It had nothing to do with fear and was beyond genetics. When one great white paw came to rest on my thigh, I looked into those blue eyes and saw Rambo, not a wolf, but still refrained from touching him. One by one the wolves disappeared into the undergrowth until there was only one left—most probably the female who called to him from the wild and saved him from the human predator. When she lifted her white muzzle to the sky and let out the most heartbreaking sound I ever heard, Rambo and all of the others answered it, but he stayed with me when she trotted off to rejoin the pack.

Dropping to my knees, I slid my arms around Rambo's neck and cried into his thick creamy fur. He allowed the affection but on Nell's approach wheeled around, immediately on the defense, snarling. I was able to get him calmed down, but for the time being, Nell kept her distance. He let me put the harness on without too much trouble but when my hand brushed over the Chi Roe tattoo, I paused. Distracted, I stared at it thinking, I understand the meaning of good fortune now but I wonder what it means to others. I don't think I've ever been more tired or jubilant. My dog was back, and he came at his own volition no matter who or what he was.

Nell and I skittered and slid down the rocks with Rambo in the lead and then drove to the cabin to meet the others. We were greeted by old Saul's pack of baying beagles who put up a fuss when they saw us. Rambo virtually ignored them and went around to the back deck with me. He walked closer to me, now trembling, with his body pressed lightly against my thigh. Everything changed when he saw Christopher. Suddenly, he was the old Rambo, leaping and dancing all around the man in a show of affection that kept the Mountaineers talking for months to come.

The sheriff's department was still assessing the damage to the cabin, taking fingerprints, scraping blood from the door jam and gathering evidence, including what was left of Grandmother's afghan. Still worried about the prints I found at the front door, I asked to speak to the sheriff. His response was to say, "Good. Let's go around to the front porch, just the two of us. We need to talk about those boot prints. I've got a hunch about 'em."

So I took him out there, showed him the enlarged photos and told him in detail exactly what I'd found, where the prints were located, and everything I could think of.

"Now, Ms. Ross, how about you taking them copies you made and layin' 'em down about where you found them if you can. I'm willin' to bet these prints will confirm what Saul says."

117

I had no idea what Saul said, but I knew what I had to offer. That was no problem since all I had to do was to find the panorama photo and let it serve as the placement guide. Reconstructing the site wasn't as easy as I expected but once the copies were stacked and arranged in order, it made sense. I could see the direction my stalker had come from, and where he paused at the bottom step, and then where he turned away at the wolf's apparent approach.

"You see up yonder?" the sheriff pointed towards a densely forested area in the distance. "These tracks agree with Saul's assessment. That's the direction our man came from, and that's where he went when he left here," he concluded, spitting tobacco juice to land next to the photos. "Hey, Saul. Can you stop talkin' long enough to come out here? I want you to see this before we go any further."

The deck talk stopped completely when Saul left. He eased around the side of the cabin to the front porch to stop and stare at the prints. "Lemme see your boot soles, Monty." Without questioning the request, the sheriff shifted to one foot, took off his boot and handed it over.

"Why that's the same as the boot stamp, only these are a lot newer," I exclaimed. "Does this mean…"

"No, it's not Monty," said the old man with a laugh. "These tracks and this mark agree with his assessment though. What we're a thinkin' is that since they're specialized and you can only get 'em at that fancy new sporting goods store over in Kingsport. It points to our man. They are a special issue just for the Carter Sheriff's Department. The rangers come under their banner."

Pointing to the arch he said, "See that mark? That stands for law enforcement in Carter County. I'm wearin' the first pair right now. I just approved them for my officers because they gave us a deep discount. They're to let me know whenever a pair sells and who bought them."

Before he went any further, the sheriff called his office. We were all in on the conversation, which he didn't even try to hide. "Yep, looks like we're onto 'em, but you aren't gonna like what I have to tell you. I'm pretty sure it's one of our own." With that, he gave his staff instructions to confirm the sale and to get back to him ASAP. Already guilty in the collective group mind, Jepson's name was prominent in the whispers that ran around the group.

"Now look here, folks, we can't condemn a man just because we suspect him. Ya'll know that. We have no proof that it's Jepson Kincaid, but I want to know where he is."

This caused some grumbling in the background, but the Sheriff was adamant. "What are you thinkin', Monty?" Saul asked.

The sheriff hesitated but finally spoke to the issue in our minds. "I'm thinking the evidence points straight at Kincaid. He's gone underground. We haven't seen him since Thanksgiving. It's lookin' bad for him if those prints really are his, but I can't touch him yet."

The look that passed between Nell and Saul spoke volumes. She cast an unforgiving eye at the sheriff. "Not even for questioning? Whose side are you on, Monty? You're giving him time to dig in deep. A tracker like him could stay up there for years without getting caught, free to terrorize that girl and everybody else. And you wonder why we take the law into our own hands."

"Now, now, Ms. Nell, don't get yourself in a huff. I'm saying we don't know where he is, and we have no absolute proof that it's him. If it turns out those prints belong to his boots, that'll be a different story." Then he turned to Christopher. "If I was you, Mr. Papadis, since she's technically your employee, I'd get Ms. Ross away from here just in case he's gone rogue. I'd say anyplace is better than here right now."

I rankled at that. The sheriff didn't even bother to ask what I thought. I was on the verge of making a heated retort when Christopher spoke. His response surprised and pleased me. "I understand what you are saying, Sheriff, but while the cabin belongs to me, and I am the residency sponsor, this is a communal project Ms. Ross is working on. Technically, Ms. Ross is her own boss. I've offered safe accommodation, but if she chooses to stay here against my wishes, it's her decision."

Irritated, the sheriff looked over at me and bumbled into territory near and dear to me. "Well, you're a fool for letting a good-looking woman like that stay up here by herself no matter who she's workin' for. It's just asking for trouble no matter how smart she is. Trouble, that's what it is."

I was silent up to that point but this was too much. "Listen, Sheriff, it's not about how I look. I have as much right to live in peace and quiet and alone if I so choose, as any man. The problem isn't me, it's men like you and Jepson Kincaid."

Nell clapped in approval while the sheriff had the grace to look uncomfortable. He kept his tail feathers close and stayed low-key for the rest of the meeting. We talked for hours about what may have happened at the cabin during the break-in and the boot tracks leading in the direction of a hidden cove just below the summit.

Before they dispersed, Saul took the floor. Superseding the sheriff, he addressed the group. "Now about them tracks. I know they're gonna match this girl's pictures, and they'll be an official issue. I'm bettin' Jepson is hid back in that cove not far from where you saw them signs. There's a shallow cave where he can shelter an' burn his cook fire without much smoke escapin'. Wildlife is plentiful so he can hunt and keep fed for a long time. The longer he stays back there, the harder it'll be to catch him. We gotta find him now, and once we find him, we'll have to bring him out into the open."

He turned to the sheriff to add, "It's real tricky back in there if Jepson's where I think he is. Almost nobody ventures there 'cause hardly anybody knows about it, and if'n they do, they can't find it. The Indians used it as a hidey place in the old days. It was one of their last. Ain't nobody been in there much since back in the thirties when a plant collector got lost in there. They like to have never found him. It's rough and overgrown with only one way in or out. You could walk past the entrance and miss it every time. Sheriff, if'n you and your men will join the Mountaineers, we can set a human net around the mouth of the cove just before dawn and flush him out. You'll have to go up on foot real quiet-like. I want ya'll to stake it out before me'n Marianna get there but you gotta be dead quiet about it in case he's out hunting early. Me'n her will go up on the old Indian trail, followin' the tree markers. Let me draw you a map."

I was so absorbed by Saul's presentation that I nearly missed the mention of my part in the strategy. Too stunned to protest, I listened closely while the old man relayed his plan for what could be the last day of my life.

"Listen here, now. I want Marianna to go in there with me and my dogs," he reiterated. Seeing the look on Christopher's face he clarified his position. "Christo, since the white one just came back from the wild, I'd appreciate it if you'd keep him with you. Don't worry; won't nuthin' harm her if she follows my directions."

After having just won a major battle for the cause of women, I felt flustered and demoted to the status of a little girl with no choices. Christopher looked like he might throw a bolt of lightning into our midst. Even the other men grumbled. Then his expression changed. He waylaid further comment by saying, "I've got it, Saul. I see where you're coming from."

Saul grinned and said, "I thought you might."

Christopher's turncoat behavior did nothing to allay my concerns. What Saul said next, however, soothed my ruffled feathers because it made sense. He turned to me saying, "I know what you're thinkin', Mari, but hear me out. I know this place better'n most, so you need to trust me like they do. We'll let these hounds of mine find our man, but you'll be the bait that brings him out. He's young, vain, and proud, so he won't be able to resist trying to get to you. That will give us the advantage of surprise. If'n we bring that wolf-dog of yours, Rambo might make a move too soon if'n he senses you are in danger. He'll try to protect you."

And all this time I thought that was what Rambo was supposed to do—protect me! Unable to speak, I stared at the man, slack-jawed with shock.

He started to walk away and then turned back to where I stood rooted to the ground, speechless and frightened half out of my mind, all thoughts of bravery abandoned.

When his face was a scant inch from mine, I could see every wrinkle, scar, and mole on it, but it was his fierce blue eyes that got me. "Don't you go chicken on me, girl. You can do this. Bring your walkin' stick, that little Glock you been practicin' with, plenty of bullets, and wear your boots. We leave at daybreak, and we'll plan to be at the mouth of the cove by mid-afternoon. Get a good night's sleep. You're gonna need it."

I quelled at the very thought of what he was asking me to do, but the more I thought about it the more sense it made. Like that blue-eyed girl in the Jack Tale, I had to confront my nemesis and take control of my fear, but first, I would take a bath and put on clean underwear.

Such was Saul's reputation that the group bowed to his wisdom about making me the bait to lure Jepson Kincaid away from his cave. I take that back. Everybody, including Nell, agreed to the plan, all except the man they called Christo. While he clearly understood the logic behind it, he wouldn't let me out of his sight, provoking sideways glances among the men.

Before the group dispersed for the night, Saul, that taciturn old man, aimed a parting shot at the ranger captain, Ransom Russell, who was still slinking in the background. "You been real quiet tonight son, and you ought to be. I know you don't want to admit it, but you made a mistake. You were warned about makin' a ranger out of Jepson Kincaid, but you wouldn't listen and did it anyway. Puttin' that troubled boy into a uniform gave him permission to strut like a rooster hereabouts, an' it set something loose that should never have been. Mari's not the only woman he's terrorized, and you know it; Stella's just the only one he's kilt so far as we know."

Embarrassed and ashamed, the ranger captain lit out of there like all the ghosts from hell were after him. We dispersed shortly after. The others followed suit, some of them glad for his discomfort. When they were all gone and Christopher and I were the only ones left behind, eyebrows were raised but none dared say a word. They just got into their trucks and left for home. I doubt Nell's truck, she was the last to leave, had reached the asphalt when Christopher Papadis took me in his arms and practically devoured my very soul with his mouth and tongue.

"I've wanted to do that all day," he whispered deep into my throat. "It's hard to believe what we've gotten into, but it makes every minute seem more important, don't you agree." He took my hand then and said, "Come."

Shivering in anticipation when he led me to the papa-bear chair, I did indeed forget everything but the moment. Rambo looked up, cocked one fuzzy eyebrow, yawned and went back to sleep in front of the fireplace, his needs apparently having been met earlier on the mountain.

Christopher settled me onto his lap where we kissed again. We had waited so long for this moment that it felt like every ticking second was a time bomb. Unbuttoning the flannel shirt, I explored under his thermals for a bit, making him groan when I pulled at the thick pelt of hair on his chest with my teeth, but he left me to it. It's not as though his hands had nothing to do.

Though tired from the day's exertions something savage awakened in me when I got to his ears. I vaguely remember hoping I wouldn't be held responsible for my actions under the circumstances. The feel of his big hands, gentle yet strong on my body, added fuel to the fire.

Eventually, we pulled apart to settle back and stare at the fire. He held me close. I clung to him in return as though this were my first and last chance to do so.

Reluctantly, he pushed me back just enough to make eye contact and spoke to the issue at hand. "There's something strange going on up here on this mountain, and I'm not at all sure it's human. Frankly, I'm not sure even the two of us could control it together if we had to.

"I can't stop thinking about how stupid I was to leave you after Rambo took off," Christopher murmured into my hair. "I know you're a strong woman, and I can understand that you value your independence, but if you'll allow it, I promise that from now on, nothing will keep me from being nearby if you want or need me."

Considering recent events, I welcomed his declaration. At that moment, however, I was far more interested in the smell of him and the feel of his hands on my breasts. "Why don't you stay," I whispered, nuzzling his neck. "I want you, and I need you."

Nothing else was necessary. By that time little beyond the present mattered to either of us anyway. We had a killer loose on Roan Mountain, but for that moment, we chose to enjoy one another.

I don't remember getting undressed, but I do remember that shower. With consummate skill, he brought me to a full-on orgasm under the force of that hot running water. I returned the favor by kneeling and taking his fullness into my mouth, touching, feeling, caressing, and driving him mad with my tongue.

The minute my head touched the pillow the man completely covered my body with his and slid into me. With a desire primal and intense, I drew him in as deep as it was possible to go. Massaging his penis with vaginal muscles primed and ready, together we exploded into a mind-numbing orgasm that seemed to go on forever. When at last we slept, it was the sleep of the near-dead. My innocence was long gone, but that night desire took me beyond sex when we literally fused and merged as one. Like the Luna Moth's mating, I wondered if either of us would survive to do it again.

*****

When Saul and the noisy beagle pack arrived at daybreak, I was dressed but groggy and sore. My dog, instinctively knowing adventure was afoot and was primed for action. He pranced around the cabin like a fidgety racehorse, but not me. I just wanted to go back to sleep. Frustrated by my lack of response, he'd do a circuit around the rooms, check on Christopher, and then come back to me, nudging my thigh with that long nose as if to say, "Come on, Mari, we've got work to do." I tried to respond appropriately but ended up taking acetaminophen to help with a lingering headache.

Considering the night before, I wasn't exactly fit for the overland trek Saul demanded of me. Christopher, who appeared rested and ready to tackle the ogre outside our door, brewed a fresh pot of coffee, brought me a cup, and took Rambo out. When he came back, I was glad that I was ready to go because Saul was with him.

"You're lookin' a bit peaked today, Missy," Saul said, glancing sideways at me. With a wicked gleam in his rheumy, old eyes, he scolded Christopher, "You should have let her get more rest last night, Christo. We got a hard day ahead of us."

124

What could we do but laugh; he had us pegged. With a sly grin on his face, that spry old mountain man took off at a brisk pace, leaving me to follow as best I could. Setting my staff forward, I forced my heavy boot-shod feet to plod on, leaving a panicked Rambo behind with Christopher, whining and barking long after the wilderness hid us from sight.

I followed Saul and his dogs, but it was without my usual vigor. Though mentally and emotionally invigorated by my night with the ardent Greek, I was distracted and my body ached in places that had been kept pristine for months.

With nowhere near enough sleep, my muscles ached for rest before we got anywhere near the Indian path. It didn't take either of us long to figure out the mission was doomed if I couldn't trek into rough territory.

"Come here, Sweetheart, I got somethin' that'll fix what's ailin' you," he said. Pulling out a dented flask of what I later found out was honest-to-god moonshine, he gave it to me with a warning. "Just a swaller, girl. Can't have you falling over your feet out here, but I don't want you drunk, neither."

Embarrassed, I'm quite sure I turned red as a blood-orange when he said that, but I took the flask, managed to smile sweetly, and said nothing.

Everything changed with the nip that he allowed me. That swig of pure mountain liquor hit me so hard it temporarily drove the night before clean out of my foggy mind with the fire coursing down my throat to swirl in my innards and down to my toes.

Coughing, I staggered around until Saul clapped me on the back a couple of times. He was right about liquor's effect because, after the stimulating adrenaline rush from the white lightning, my body basically cooperated with me. This was a good thing since a perpetual orgasm had simmered on the back burner ever since we left the cabin, aching for release and serving to distract me. After determining that I would live, we took to the trail again where I was able to better follow in the old man's wake. I couldn't afford to let Saul down, not out here on the mountain. As my grandmother might have said, "It just wouldn't do."

The path we eventually connected to was rougher and steeper than any I had trekked since coming to upper East Tennessee. Blending completely into the forest surrounding, it was the first marker tree, its trunk bent as a malleable sapling long ago, that directed us to the invisible path. Although the way was barely navigable, somehow Saul and his dogs forged ahead with confidence, leaving me to follow in their tracks.

It didn't take long to become aware that I was in a strange and wonderful place. Massive trees and thick vines kept morning's sun at bay long after daylight emerged elsewhere. The ground was slick with layers of damp leaves, moss, and lichen. Had I not been on a deadly mission, I would have found it fascinating.

Chapter 9

Saul and I hiked until well into the afternoon, taking breaks only for personal stops and to sip water. Never in my life had I trekked like that, and while I enjoyed being out with the master tracker, the fear which rode my back grew heavier by the minute. The closer we got to the cove, my thoughts of Christopher were gradually replaced by worries about what I might face in a confrontation with Kincaid, if that's truly who he was.

I wore the Glock under the shoulder in the neat leather holster Nell had given. "Your pocket is no place to have a gun in an emergency. Wear this and get used to having it at hand and not having to feel around for it," she told me. That made sense at the time, and now I was glad for the advice.

If I liked or approved of guns in the first place, wearing that holster with a loaded gun might have felt natural. As it was, I knew it was for the purpose of kill or be killed and that frightened me. *How will I react if I need to use it?* I asked myself. But I had no answers. I had never shot to wound or kill anything and did not relish the thought of doing so now.

The sun was directly overhead when we made the entrance to the cove, but walking into it, the light dimmed significantly. I had no idea of the elevation in that little valley, but Roan Mountain is over six thousand feet, and we were not far from the grassy bald peak. We were up there. Inside that hidden cove to which there was only one entrance, was a primeval forest untouched by modernity's saw. The trees were big, gnarled and very, very old. Had I not been on a mission, I would have loved to explore its environs. As it was, we had work to do.

*****

Some distance away, mountaineers and local law enforcement were forming an invisible human cage around the cove's lone entrance, but it gave me little reassurance. In spite of the beauty, the place held an aura of danger, almost as though something sinister permeated the air.

With nothing more than a hand signal, Saul communicated with his dogs while I rested my aching legs. The spry mountaineer knelt in their midst, holding a shirt of Kincaid's that they sniffed eagerly, white-tipped tails waving. When he stood up again and gave an almost imperceptible signal, they took off in pursuit of a trail only they could find. He kept White Tail, the pack leader with us.

Why did he let the others go and keep just one here with us?

As though he read my mind, Saul looked up and said, "The pack'll find our man an' this ole' boy will lead us to them. He'll take over from there. Can't nothing hide from a beagle," he told me, even though I'd said not a word, "especially not White Tail."

Saul seemed in no rush to follow his dogs which allowed me to rest a bit longer. He leaned back against the boulder with the grizzled old beagle at his feet and stared hard at me before he spoke.

"You got a lot of gumption for a city girl. Not many would have come into this wilderness to catch a crazy man with me."

I stared back at him, thinking hard about what I should say. I was totally unprepared for what came next. "I wanted you to come today because I know you still see Stella's dead body in your dreamtime, ain't that right?"

At my nod, he went on. I'm sorry about that woman gettin' herself killed. Nobody deserves what she had to go through, but it's a real shame you had to find her like that."

Mute, I let his words settle into my psyche. It was quiet in the forest with minimal birdsong, though I expected a chorus of sound. What I remember most is a gentle wind whispering through giant trees, millions

128

of shades of green, enormous fern fronds, mushrooms, and the subliminal sound of a creek nearby. In this darkest of green places, moss covered the rocks and trees like a silent cloak that the forest wrapped around me. For the briefest moment, I felt comforted.

"It's just like in the story Nell told you. That girl had to face the evil spirit to get free of the curse. You gotta face the man who killed Stella and who now threatens you. You gotta get rid of that picture of her that's playin' in your head, or at least put it on a shelf you don't have to look at all the time. What you saw will haunt you if'n you don't, and his power over you will increase."

Saul watched my face while the cacophony of what I felt played there, uncovered. He waited until he thought I was ready, then continued. "We want you to stay up here, Mari, be a permanent part of our mountain community if you will, but not if'n you ain't happy to be here. Not if'n you see that body every time you turn around, livin' in fear because Jepson Kincaid ain't been brought down."

Up to that time, I thought of Saul as a quiet, reclusive man. Now I knew him as a sage, a shaman of sorts who spoke wisdom when necessity demanded it. I nodded, put my tough bamboo stick to the ground, and pushed off from the rocks. Saul followed me until the pack set to at full voice.

Dense foliage muffled their call, distorting the sound. "They've found something. Don't you worry none, White Tail will take us to 'em," he said, releasing the dog.

The beagle wasted no time taking off after the pack full steam ahead with a full-throated bay, tail up, ears flying. It was as though everything in the forest went into motion with him. Trees swayed, rabbits and squirrels raced, white-tail deer jumped over downed trees, a cougar leaped a stream nearby.

"You ready for this?" asked the old man, his rheumy, old eyes twinkling with excitement. "Stay with me. I don't want you to get hurt, not after all we been through. Besides, Christo would kill me, an' I ain't ready to go just yet. By the way, they're here. I saw signs."

I had no time to consider where our people were or to ponder his words. In the distance, we could hear Jepson Kincaid holler over the dogs, "Gettum' off of me! Call the dogs off for God's sake!"

Saul caught me then, saying, "I want you to keep him distracted. For God's sake, stay close to me. Get that gun out and be damned careful with it. We want that bugger alive."

About a half-mile into the small, secluded pocket of dark primeval forest, we found our man backed up against the wall of a low, nearly invisible opening in the rock face. No longer cocky and sure of himself, Kincaid cowered at the dogs' vocal aggression. Unkempt and unshaven, Kincaid looked and acted like a wild man until he spied me. Then his entire demeanor changed. He still cringed at the dogs' presence, but he stood up straighter to glare at me through bloodshot, crazed eyes. Saul, with his rifle cocked and aimed squarely at the man, saw the transition Kincaid made when I did and moved forward to stand in front of me.

"So they brought you, girlie! Don't try to hide behind that old man—come out and face me." Unable to help myself, I craned around Saul and his big floppy hat until I made eye contact. With a wicked grin, Kincaid resumed his rant, virtually slamming me against a brick wall. "I was still there when you found Stella, you know—heard you and the white wolf-dog come up the deer trail. That's why the buzzards were still up in the air. If you hadn't had the dog with you, your body would have joined Stella's in that pit. I'd have played with it first like I did hers." Involuntarily, I stepped back at the venom in his voice.

Kincaid spoke again, his voice silky, almost caressing my fear with his tongue. "Scared, ain't you? Well, you ought to be. As long as I'm on my feet, my hands are free, and there ain't no bullet through my skull, I can still get to you one way or another. I'm not finished with you, not by a longshot."

He giggled then, an other-worldly sound that made my stomach twist into knots. I took another step back, and Kincaid, seeing my inadvertent response, bunched up as if to make a move. I suddenly understood the king cobra's power and wanted to collapse where I stood, thinking, *We're living the story of the evil spirit.*

Saul, who'd kept the dogs on full alert since they seemed to be the only thing Kincaid feared, interrupted the tirade. "You just stay where you are Jepson Kincaid. Ain't no way you can get at her. Besides, we got company. Look around you, boy."

Nell and the rugged mountaineers, sheriff's deputies, rangers, and one snow white German shepherd accompanied by Christopher Papadis emerged from the forest, shoulder to shoulder. It was at that moment that Kincaid, ignoring the dogs and the guns we held, pushed away from the wall to come at me. The move was so quick and so unexpected that when his body knocked Saul's aside and crashed into mine, I collapsed under the assault.

Thrashing beneath Kincaid's angry pummeling, I gasped for air. In response, he pressed his face closer to mine with an evil grin. My gut rebelled against his rancid breath and the crazed eyes boring into mine. Strong dirty fingers wrapped around my neck and squeezed.

Like in science-fiction, I saw Christopher in my mind's eye, saw the fury and felt the action before he made it. What came next was almost unimaginable. Faster than the eye could track, dog and man propelled themselves through the air to hit Kincaid in a full body slam and push him away from me.

Fueled by incredible combined energy, all three flew to the back of the shallow cave in a violent confrontation. In the end, Kincaid lay on the floor unable to move beneath the weight of my dog. The triumphant Rambo stayed where he was, teeth bared and saliva dripping onto the man's face, keeping him pinned to the ground. His face masked by a black cloud of fury, Christopher pulled away from them to help Saul and me get up and out of the way.

The sheriff and his deputies took over from there, but Kincaid wasn't finished with me. Passing within spitting distance, Kincaid's angry eyes sought mine. "Ain't no jail can hold the likes of me. I'll find you, Bitch, you and that damned foreigner. But before I kill you, I will do stuff to you that will make you wish you could die faster. Ain't no place this side of hell you can hide from me until I'm dead, and even then, I'll haunt you."

I heard him but I didn't believe it.

*****

Later that night, Christopher and I lay in bed discussing what we'd seen and heard. We were both bruised and scraped, but he seemed incredibly tired. An air of melancholy clung to him, and he seemed distant. Unsure of his response, I ventured to ask him about what I'd seen when he and Rambo attacked Kincaid.

"I still can't believe that move you and Rambo made."

He was silent for a time as though pondering what to say. When he spoke, his voice was rough with emotion.

"I can't really explain it, Mari, partly because I'm afraid it'll sound like something from a comic book. It's as though a bizarre energy consumes me when somebody or something I care about is threatened."

"But that's not unusual," I said, interrupting him. "We all get adrenaline rushes."

"I know that, but this feels different. It's almost as though the rush transforms into a tsunami. You saw what happened with Kincaid when he attacked you."

To be truthful, what I saw was anything but normal, however, I wasn't put off by it. I wanted to know more. "So, when was the first time it happened?"

It was odd to see such a self-assured man hesitate like that, but it was obvious the topic was difficult. When he finally began to talk, he told me a strange story, but it helped me to understand him better.

"A child without siblings, I had a black and white border collie for a companion. He was my best friend, confidant, and protector, and we went almost everywhere together. One day we were out on a trail when a pack of wild dogs attacked. Of course, Mutt—that's what I called him—went on the defense and drew them away, but there were too many for one small dog to fight. From out of nowhere came the most intense anger I'd ever known, but instead of a flare of temper, it felt more like a rod of cold steel ran through me. Instead of running, I waded into the fray, cast the strays aside in bloody disarray, and took Mutt home to get help. When my mother asked about the attack, I described it to her, but not my part in it. Mutt died that night. I later got another dog, but nothing erased the memory of that experience from my mind."

"But up there on that mountain, did you know the power would come to our aid? Can you draw on it at will?"

"Apparently not," he said with a chuckle. "Look, I'm no superman but when Kincaid slandered you and then attacked, the steel rod in my spirit turned molten hot, forcing me to act. That it happened in concert with Rambo gives food for speculation. It makes me wonder if there's a mystical connection to certain animals in our family's heritage that has passed down to me."

Not for the first time, I wondered at his old-world speech patterns and speculated if perhaps he was dealing with something far more ancient and godlike than anger. Little frightened him, but for someone he loved, there were no boundaries he would not cross.

What I knew for certain was that it bothered him to be out of control.

Before sleep, he turned to me with an expression of profound sadness. "I care deeply for you, but are you willing to risk something like this again?" I think my response satisfied him because we both slept soundly into the next day.

*****

Later in the week, Christopher and I went to dinner at Jonesborough's premier Greek-American restaurant, The Black Olive.

"So how does this food compare to what you know of Greek food?" I asked him.

"It's not my mother's cooking, for sure," he said with a smile, "but it tastes just fine. We'd love you to come to dinner at her home in Elizabethton soon. She'd like to meet you, and then you could judge for yourself."

This was the second time he'd mentioned my going to his mother's place, and this time I was willing to consider the invitation. We ate a leisurely dinner surrounded by people I didn't know. Not that it mattered, really, but the recent notoriety had begun to get to me. There were probably some diners there who recognized us from the papers and television, but they were unwilling to intrude on our time together.

That night I began to really know more about Christopher Papadis. He began with telling me about his childhood, of coming to the mountains of upper East Tennessee after college graduation, and of deciding to make this place his home.

"The family home is in Woodfin near Asheville, North Carolina. Growing up, my dad was gone a lot, but my mom was a typical Greek mother. She stayed home and made sure I was loved, fed, and taken care of. Between mom and dad when he was home, and Otto my tutor, I was as secure as any son of immigrants could ask for. How about you?"

"Not nearly as warm and friendly as your growing up was," I said with a slight frown. "I had a strong fundamentalist father who expected his wife to raise me, keep house, be active in the church, and have a home-cooked meal on the table at 6:00 p.m. He wanted me to follow in Mom's footsteps—get a good education and then either teach or work as a secretary until I married and had kids."

I looked down, thinking about the choices I'd made, and what dad would think of the man sitting across from me. It was then that I saw the softness in Christopher's eyes and knew I could tell him more.

"Dad and I failed to see eye-to-eye on most things." Talking to him was so natural and easy that I found myself telling him more than I planned. "He worried that I would go to hell unless I got saved, but I just couldn't buy it. I think it broke his heart but I couldn't pretend to be something I wasn't. There was life to live out there, and I wanted to try it on my own."

"And what did that life turn out to be?" he asked over cannoli and coffee.

"Oh, I went to college and got the degree, but working nine to five just didn't suit. Instead, I took a job with the local arts journal and spent the next four years with them. I later moved to the weekly newspaper which had a broader circulation. My situation was better there and the pay was certainly an improvement but everything changed when we got a new editor-in-chief. I let him tie me down for another two years until we broke up. Then your letter came, and I flew away with a free heart and my mom's blessing."

"But not your dad's?"

"He passed away just before I graduated from college. It's probably a good thing he doesn't know everything I've done. He'd have a fit if he knew I was living in a cabin in the woods without a man to protect me. And he'd surely have concerns about you!"

I looked up to catch him in a wolfish smile, but he said nothing more. We were preparing to leave when my phone rang. Normally I wouldn't have answered, but it was from my mom.

"Mom, are you okay?" I asked, but it wasn't my mother's voice that I heard. "Mari, it's Jason. Your mother is ill and at Tallahassee Memorial Hospital in serious condition. How soon can you get here?"

"What do you mean she's ill? What's happened, and why are you calling to tell me about it? Let me talk to her."

"Listen, Mari, she's in ICU here in Tallahassee with an acute pancreatic condition. The doctors are trying to get the pain under control, and she can't talk right now."

My romantic evening with Christopher fell into shambles since all I could think of was my mother and why it had to be Jason who called to tell me she was in the hospital. Would I never be rid of him?

Though I loved Tennessee's oldest town with its stepped roofline architecture and brick streets, there had been little time to explore it up till then, nor would there be that night. Now I had to leave it in a hurry, but most of my possessions were on Roan Mountain in the cabin with Rambo. Christopher assured me everything would be safe and that he would take care of Rambo if I wanted to book a flight from Johnson City's airport.

I wanted to get home quickly and was able to get a flight booked online, so I left Tennessee without makeup, a change of clothing or fresh underwear.

On the way, I called Nell to ask if she'd share dogsitting duties with Christopher while I was away. Not only did she agree, but she promised to drive up to the cabin, pick Rambo up, and take him back to her place until Christopher could come back for him. That was a relief because even with Jepson Kincaid in jail, new locks, and a security system, I still hated leaving Rambo alone.

If life could go to hell in a handbasket twice in one week, that's what mine did after Jason's call. We flew down I-26 at a breakneck speed in an effort to get me to the airport in time for the last-minute flight. Why we failed to attract attention from the highway patrol is beyond me, but we made it to Blountville in time with no problem.

I gave Christopher a quick peck on the cheek, then flew out of the truck like a banshee on a mission, checked in at the kiosk, got my boarding pass, and then literally ran to the security check-in line. Breathing hard by that time I fumbled with my shoes and jewelry, I managed to pass through metal detection unscathed.

The Johnson City Airport is relatively compact, so it didn't take long to scoot down the escalator to my gate, but the waiting after that is what I found difficult. Nervous as a cat I sat there crossing and uncrossing my legs, cracking my knuckles, and chewing my lip until they finally allowed us to board the plane.

I couldn't make it fly faster but I wanted to. The flight from Tri-Cities only takes about twenty minutes, but we had to circle Atlanta. Then I had to race through multiple levels, hit the people-mover and access the underground before emerging to find the gate bound for Tallahassee. I made it just in time for boarding. Then my luck changed. Flight delay—birds on the runway the sign said.

It was early evening when I finally arrived in Tallahassee. By that time, I suspected that driving twelve hours might have been less stressful. Renting a car, I headed straight for Tallahassee Memorial, the hospital in which I was born, where my dad died, and now where my mom struggled for life.

Besides worry for her, I had a sick sense of foreboding in the pit of my stomach, approaching the hospital parking garage. Surely Mom and Jason hadn't hooked up when I left for Tennessee. They always liked one another and bantered with the ease of old friends but to my knowledge, nothing more. Was he her companion at Thanksgiving, and was that why she hedged at telling me? What was I supposed to do if they had?

Jason was waiting for me when I arrived at the ICU. Interestingly enough, my senses detected only worry and concern and that made it easier to deal with him.

"Thanks for calling me," I told him. "What happened?"

"Your mom took a bad turn night before last, and yesterday it got so bad we called 911."

"Excuse me for asking, but why did she call you instead of me?"

He had the grace to looked discomfited but answered me nonetheless. "Look, I know what you're thinking, but there's really nothing between your mom and me but friendship. We were platonic friends when you and I were together—that didn't change just because we broke up. Take it or leave it, but that's the truth. As for not calling you, she thought it was heartburn or something. Thinking it would get better, she didn't call you because of everything that was already on your plate. When they took her to the hospital and things escalated, she asked me—"

"—I still don't understand, Jason."

"Okay, so I was with her when she had the attack. We'd gone to dinner and just got home when it started. I stayed with her all night and finally convinced her to let me call 911."

"And?" I was not going to let him off the hook. We were almost to the ICU, and I needed answers before I walked in there.

"When you left, she was fine for a while, all the way through Thanksgiving, actually. Then Cassie got hold of it and started calling her, telling lies about seeing me with other women and getting her all worked up. Then I backed off. I couldn't take Cassie either. We'd just made up, and I thought things were going well until she got sick that night. My take on it is that her body finally had all it could take and turned on her."

Something stirred in the back of my mind when he said that about Cassie. It was the picture of her sitting backlit at the restaurant before I left for Tennessee, the time she berated me and I had thought her hair was on fire.

Jason, seeing that I had drifted away, broke into my thoughts. "Mari, If I were you, I'd block that woman from coming up here or calling. I don't have that authority, or I would have done it sooner. She's flat out crazy."

When he said that, into my mind unbidden came the demonic face of Jepson Kincaid. He and Cassie were two of a kind. God only knows what would happen if they got together.

I had to wonder what was going on. Until very recently my life had been dull, reliably so. Now I was confronted by erratic and potentially dangerous personalities. My ex-boyfriend was taking care of my seriously ill mom, perhaps a little too well; my former best friend was obviously off her rocker, and a crazy man still wanted to kill me. What else could happen?

There were no easy answers to be had and no quick fix for any of it.

*****

At triage, Jason introduced me to the charge nurse who then led me to my mother's room. Thank goodness she had it to herself because I don't think I could have handled being polite to strangers just then. We entered through a wall of glass doors to find Mom drawn up into a ball with her eyes shut tight. She was hooked up to several machines, her hair loosely drawn up into a sloppy bun with not a shred of makeup on her face. This was not the glamorous mother I left behind a scant three months earlier. This was a stranger.

Not to be overly melodramatic, but had not Jason been there to catch me, I might have collapsed in shock. But he was there. and he stood with me, a look of intense concern for my mother on his face.

Finally becoming aware that we were there, she frowned, let out a loud sigh and opened her eyes. When she saw it was me, those big eyes widened in surprise. "It's you, my baby," she said, holding her hand out to touch my cheek. "I thought the nurse was here to give me another injection." Then she turned to Jason and in mock severity fussed at him. "What have you done? I told you not to call Mari, but you did it anyway!"

For the first time in a long while I can honestly say that I really appreciated him. He was there when she needed him, called me when it became necessary, and stuck by her. That sense of responsibility spoke to me on several levels so that I looked at him through new lenses. As a result, I began to accept what had to be done with calm instead of reacting to everything he said and did.

"Oh, Mom, thank goodness he called," I told her. "Pancreatitis is nothing to be trifled with."

She looked frail and sounded worse, so I had to lean close to hear the rest. "Mari, I'm just so glad you're here. I wanted to see you and make sure you were all right, but I didn't want to call. You had enough on your plate from what I could tell."

"Aw, Ma, you know me. I always bounce back when life smacks me around just like you do. You can always call me."

"I am well aware of that," she said with a half-smile at the endearment, but it ended in a grimace of pain. "I was also worried about what you'd think if you found out Jason and I were still friends. Don't worry. I won't ever repeat the stupid escapade from several years ago. Jason is dear to me, but I am not attracted to him in that way."

I wasn't at all sure about that, but it seemed to me she was talking too much, almost babbling. The truth is that when my mom has something on her mind, God forbid I should interrupt, so leaning closer, I let her ramble.

"There's something wrong with Cassie, dear. I can't put my finger on it, but she's turned. When I'm around her there's a distinct feeling of unrest and evil intent." She saw the look on my face and drew me closer and whispered. "I'm not being dramatic, Mari. She's hurt me, damaged my relationship with Jason and even tried to finagle information about you out of me. I believe it's an insane kind of jealousy, so you'd best be careful. She's out for blood, but I cannot imagine why."

"Sure Mom, I'll be careful," I told her, saying anything to placate her. "I sensed something was going on with Cassie before I left. You get some rest now and let me go out to the desk to see if I can find out more about what's going on."
She nodded and was asleep before I could leave the room. Jason merely nodded and resumed his watch at the door when I passed him.

The nurse had little to add beyond the preliminary diagnosis but the doctor wanted to run more tests. We went over mom's medical history, and that of our family, looking for possible causes, and the treatment modalities the doctor ordered. I asked when he might come in and learned that it would be early the following morning.

"Jason, why don't you go home and get some rest now," I told him. "I'm here, and I want to be in this room when her doctor makes the rounds first thing tomorrow."

Obviously exhausted, he didn't protest overmuch. Before leaving he reminded me once again to be on guard against Cassie. "Look, I know you think we're overreacting to Cassie but—"

I interrupted him mid-sentence. "—Oh, I believe every word you're saying. We had a couple of run-ins with my leaving the paper and taking the residency. She was most unhappy with my choices but instead of simply saying so, her responses were vehement and accusatory. I still can't believe how she's acted since then, especially to my mom. It's not like my old friend at all."

When he left us, the room fell silent with only mom's faint snore in the background and the occasional 'swoosh' when she got an automatic dose of morphine. The whole thing was so surreal that I could hardly believe any of this was happening. In a way, it served to distract me from the recent trauma on Roan Mountain.

At daybreak, my phone vibrated, waking me from a deep sleep in the recliner. "Hello?" The phone was silent for a moment, but then I heard a gravelly female voice that I knew and missed. Nell. Struggling to wake up, I fumbled for the phone and then made my way out to the corridor.

Instead of greeting me, she said, "I hate to be the bearer of bad news girl, but somebody's got to do it."

Deep dread ran through me when I answered, "Tell me what? Is it Christopher? Rambo? Nell, what's wrong?"

"That good-for-nuthin' bastard, Jepson Kincaid, broke out of jail. They should've put it on top of him, but no, he was 'a good ole' home boy—he wouldn't try to get away.' I tried to tell 'em he was smart. Not wise, just smart and cunning like a fox."

My world went dark and time stopped. "Did you just tell me Jepson Kincaid broke out of jail?"

"He did that and more. One of his cousins called to say he's on his way to Florida to pick you off, too." She paused before continuing. "Child, have you still got that Glock?"

"No. There was no time to go back for the gun or anything else. Besides, since I flew down here, security would have taken it anyway." Nell cursed at that, but there wasn't much I could say since I was having trouble breathing. Jepson Kincaid was coming after me.

There was little more she could tell me except that Christopher was keeping Rambo close by his side and planning to come south to be with me. That helped somewhat, but I couldn't get the nagging sense of worry off my mind. Jepson Kincaid was after me, and I was in a hospital with my seriously ill mother and hundreds of other sick people, staff, and visitors. Unless Sheriff Monty had already notified the Tallahassee Police Department, we had no protection whatsoever.

At first, I went into panic mode until my sanity resumed its usual frenetic level and I was able to think with a reasonably clear head.

My first task was to alert hospital security to let them know what was happening but no sooner had the police major arrived than the doctor came in. They clashed immediately and things went into an uproar when the doctor ordered security to back off and to wait outside the door. Knowing a killer was potentially approaching, the police major demanded a presence in the room for safety's sake. Compromise finally reached, guards were posted immediately outside the glass doors, at the stairs and elevators on that floor. We drew the curtains and tried to settle down and pay attention to Dr. Casson, who was still in a huff.

Frankly, I was in turmoil, too. Mom looked vulnerable and incredibly fragile in her hospital bed. I had come to help, but instead, great danger trailed in my wake. Nothing I'd experienced up to that point frightened me as much as this. None of the people in that little room with its drapes and machines had any idea what I saw in Jepson Kincaid's eyes in that remote cave. I couldn't get it off of my mind. Worse, Rambo and Christopher were well over 600 miles to the north of me. Taking a deep breath, I forced my mind to compartmentalize and focus on Dr. Casson's assessment of my mother's condition.

"Our tests confirmed you had an acute pancreatic attack, Mrs. Ross, but there's something else going on in there. We'll need to do a biopsy on it before I can discharge you."

I thought Mom's eyes were going to roll back in her head over that piece of information. We both knew what it could mean—cancer—but she refused to acknowledge the possibility.

"Let me go home, for God's sake," she snapped at him. "My mother had attacks like this throughout her life. She survived them, and I will, too."

Unperturbed by her fretfulness, Dr. Casson turned the full force of his authority on her. "I understand what you're saying, Mrs. Ross. It's not my intention to get you upset or to dispute your mother's experience, but the pictures we took clearly show a spot on your pancreas that should not be there. This is serious, ma'am."

Fright aged her lovely face for a fraction of a moment, showing deep lines where none had been moments earlier. "Oh, go away you old busybody," she snapped back. "You'd see anything that would make a buck." Not a little embarrassed, she transformed into a sulky Southern belle, looking up at him with contrite eyes. "Oh, I'm just so irritable. You'll have to forgive me for being out of sorts, Dr. Casson but I simply cannot accept it. There can't be anything seriously wrong with me. this will pass; it always does."

"Not this time, ma'am." Just as he turned to gauge my response to Mom's unexpected outburst one of the guards phoned in to let us know Jason and another visitor were there.

At the moment, my attention had to be on my mother so I asked them to wait and turned back to her. Taking her hand, I tried to soothe her into agreeing to the tests "Mother, we love you and don't want to see you in this kind of pain. Tell me, has it ever been this bad before?"

"Let me put it this way, Mrs. Ross," said the doctor, breaking in with a severe expression on his face, "if you want to continue with these attacks unabated, that's your choice. If you'd prefer not to know you have cancer you can ignore that, too, but I can't. You're too vital to give up so easily. Please let me run the tests, all of them."

I could tell from the look on my mother's face that at first, she enjoyed the interchange. I was also watching when cold reality struck home. She flinched and nearly doubled over in the bed from pain. When it passed, Mom straightened up and then leaned back against the pillow before speaking. When she did, it was to look her medico in the eye and challenge him to make her well.

"Go for it, Doctor. Run the tests."

Obviously relieved that his patient would comply but blissfully unaware of the potential for danger, Dr. Casson nodded, smiled at us, and tried to take himself away. He was obviously startled when he walked into the phalanx of law enforcement officers and two very concerned-looking men who tried to file into the room at his exit.

His demeanor changed from vague to immediate concern. "Why are you still here? The people on this floor are critically ill and are not to be disturbed."

The charge nurse quickly pulled him aside to explain what she knew about the situation, but he was inflexible. Mom was his patient and in his willful arrogance, he meant to protect her health no matter what happened to anyone else.

"Ms. Ross is welcome at any time but you are not to allow more than one other visitor into that room at any given time, understood? The security guards will stay out here. My patient is not to be disturbed."

Her jaw hardened at the volley he spat out, but the nurse followed his instructions to the letter. Shortly thereafter, the two guards stayed outside Mom's room to watch the hallway while Jason went in to sit with her.

Our other guest turned out to be Christopher. Oblivious to heads swiveling our direction, I grabbed him as though he were the only man left standing.

"Did you drive?" I whispered into his neck, refusing to let go.

"Yes. We left early this morning. I came straight here."

"You know Jepson broke jail and is on his way here. May actually be here as we speak."

He drew me away from the guards and down the hall before speaking again. "Nell and I left as soon as we found out. She's with

143

Rambo at the La Quinta. No way could we let you go through this alone. If Kincaid's here, he'll get more than he bargained for."

"But there's more, Christopher. My old friend Cassie has been harassing my mother. I'm beginning to think there's some kind of connection."

Before he could respond, I was summoned to the security office on the second floor.

The Tallahassee Police Department major, two officers, and the hospital's head of security escorted us with two in front and two behind. We made quite a spectacle, garnering attention through the halls and down the elevator. I wanted to ask about Rambo, Nell, and Saul but somehow this didn't seem to be the time for talk. Instead, when Christopher put his arm around my shoulder, I leaned into him and drew comfort from his solid presence.

Looking back on it now, I realized it was the first time we were a couple like that. I found Stella's body, and he found me. We faced Jepson Kincaid together several times, a terrible storm, my illness, and then made the most exquisite love exactly once, but not until that moment had he simply 'been there' with me. Learning to walk in sync took some practice but we soon found the rhythm that would eventually become as natural as breathing.

A selfish thought crossed my mind that in trying to be a good daughter, I'd brought a terrible crisis to my hometown, but at least I wasn't alone.

"In here, Ms. Ross," said the hospital's head of security, opening the door. At first, she wanted to prevent Christopher's entry until I convinced her that he knew as much as I did about Jepson Kincaid and maybe more.

We spent the better part of the morning telling the police major what we knew and what happened to us in Tennessee. I even ventured to tell her about Cassie's strange behavior. She frowned at that, indicating it surely had nothing to do with Kincaid's mission to kill me. By that time, I wasn't so sure.

I had no idea what to think because everything around me was surreal and unexpected, even my mother's illness, Jason's role in her life, and now Christopher here with me in Tallahassee. I was sure of only three things at that moment: I wanted to protect my mom and keep her safe; I wanted all of us to survive the coming storm; and I wanted Christopher Papadis by my side forever.

Chapter 10

At the end of our interview with Major Younger, we were assigned a security detail and instructed to avoid Mom's house in Blairstone Forest since it was an obvious target. We were to be accompanied by two deputies at all times and driven to and from the hospital in a secure vehicle. It was a given that I would stay with Christopher.

When we got back to Mom's room, Jason came out to greet us. Since it was the first time I'd spent time with him since leaving Tallahassee, I had to wonder what my response would be, but I felt virtually nothing. Perhaps it was because I was so secure in my relationship with Christopher. It still seems odd how comfortable the two men were together. They were about the same height but the similarity ended there. Christopher was ruggedly handsome and had the tawny skin and dark eyes of his European ancestors. Jason was fair-skinned with black hair and hazel eyes. He may have been the elder of the two but Christopher appeared the most self-assured.

Mom's eyes widened when she met Christopher. For the briefest moment, my guard flew up but there was no need. He greeted her as one God might to a Goddess and captured her heart. Had Mom not been so sick, I'm sure that she would have been mortified by her appearance, but in spite of it, she still managed a bit of the coquette in her greeting to my handsome Greek. In response, he pulled out the most courtly of old-world manners imaginable, captivating her before she knew she'd been snared.

That they were both masters of the art of communication was obvious. Christopher held her tiny hand in his big one and quietly told her what a wonderful daughter she'd raised and about the work I was doing for the Lord Papadis Foundation and the people of Roan Mountain. She hung on every word that came out of his mouth, pleased to hear that her daughter was up to the task she'd taken on.

Far more difficult was telling her about Jepson Kincaid and the danger we were in. Instead of panic over the possibility of a mad man attacking us at the hospital, she responded in a harsh whisper, "Oh, my God. So that's why there are guards outside my door. Cassie was right. You went up there to craft a new life for yourself and found trouble. Now, look what's happened." Then, "What on earth are we supposed to do?"

I can't say that I was pleased with the reference to Cassie's prediction and said as much, but it did little to assuage her fears.

"Marianna, I feel so helpless and vulnerable," she complained. "I'm worried about you and Christopher. You shouldn't be here."

"I know how you feel, Mom. I'm just sorry I brought this nightmare with me," I told her. "I can't understand why I mean so much to him or what I did to make him so angry in the first place. What I do know is that it began the day Rambo and I arrived on the mountain and got worse the longer I stayed. Then I found Stella in that shallow pit and it all went south. When I left Tennessee, I thought that man was locked up tight. It never dawned on me that he might break out for the purpose of following me here."

We spent the rest of the day at the hospital with my mom. Jason came after work, so Christopher stayed with her while Jason and I took a quick trip to the cafeteria for a chat.

"Jason, thank you for bringing Mom to the hospital and for being so attentive to her. It looks like she had a close call, and if you hadn't been there, I don't know what would have happened to her." Pausing for effect, I had this scenario carefully planned out, I looked up to ask him a blunt-force question. "Are you and my mother having an affair?"

He looked stunned by the question, so much so that he answered honestly. "I do love her, Mari."

White hot anger flooded through me. I pushed it back, ready for rapid departure but just as quickly he caught my hand and held me there until I was willing to listen. "Don't run off like an upset child. Let me finish. I remember the stories you told me about her flirtations in the past. This is different."

A quick retort flew out of my mouth. "Listen, when I quit the paper, it was pretty clear you were already with Melinda, so why not my mom, too? Why should you be any different; she's had others." The look on his face told me I finally had his attention, so I continued to clean out my storehouse of grievances. "Couldn't you wait until I was out the door to make it obvious?"

What could he say? I spoke the truth, and he knew it. "I know what you're saying, and it's true. Melinda had been after me ever since I got to the paper, so I turned to her. Besides, it was a way to get back at you. She meant nothing more to me than as a way to make you jealous and to make me feel that I could still deliver. On a slightly different note, I'm not involved romantically with your mother, but I'd like to be."

I turned to stare at him, eyebrows raised. Had he been listening to himself he might have understood my skepticism.

"Let's get back to the core of the matter. I didn't say that I was 'in love' with your mom, did I? But I do love her, and if she'd allow it, I'd make her mine in a heartbeat, older than me, sick or not."

That got my attention. I just assumed that she was a quickie challenge for his list of conquests and that he was yet another of her affairs.

"Your mom was really kind to me when you and I were dating. She even held my hand when you adopted that white dog, kicked me out, and then took off for Tennessee. She is still good to me, and I would do anything for her."

Jason sat back and watched my tail feathers settle with a self-satisfied grin on his face. *He knows me too well,* I thought.

He went back to see Mom while I stayed behind to chew on fragments of our conversation. I wondered if I could tolerate this new development with my mother or if I had any choice in the matter.

I was still digesting the conversation with Jason when Christopher settled into the chair across from mine. He set a bag of aromatic cinnamon bagels and cream cheese in front of me. I was so deep in my own thoughts that, for once, his presence barely registered.

Unwilling to let me stay in that dark place, he broke in, passing a cup of fresh brew under my nose. "Staring at a cup of cold coffee will get you nowhere." When I failed to answer, he leaned over the small table, took my face in his, and kissed me lightly. "Earth to Marianna Ross. Please respond."

Inhaling the scent of good coffee, I looked up and smiled, but the pleasure didn't last long.

"Dr. Casson wants you to know he's scheduled an MRI for your mom tomorrow morning."

"So he feels it's that urgent? I just wonder how they're supposed to get her down to the imaging center if Kincaid's still on the loose," I told him. "It's really unfortunate that we don't have an invisibility cloak to hide under."

"I can't stop thinking there are too many loose ends, some of them floating around here. First, my former best friend Cassie goes certifiably crazy, prophesying doom and gloom and planting fears into Mom's head. Then Mom falls seriously ill, so I fly home, leaving my guard dog behind. When I get here, it's to find my former live-in boyfriend hovering over Mom like a sick mother hen. Then the man who has sworn to kill me escapes from jail and is now hot on my trail. So how does that sound? Should I be concerned or what?"

Christopher paused to think before answering, "It's true, trouble is sticking to you, but I cannot see the force behind it."

Though his comment was odd, sounding mystical to my ear, I found a measure of comfort in Christopher's strange words even though there were no answers in them.

"So tell me, where is Rambo?" I asked again. "Still with Nell at the hotel?"

He nodded and we began the long winding walk back to Intensive Care, trailed by our guard. "He knows something is up because he paces around the room constantly and stops at the door on every turn."

Mom was alone in her room when we got back. "I hope you ate something, Mari," she said with motherly concern. I took that to mean she was feeling better. "I sent Jason home. He's been here with me off and on for the past several days, and he needs his rest."

Resisting the urge to roll my eyes I leaned into Christopher and whispered, "See how she talks about him? I'm positive there's more going on here than meets the eye." I waited to tell him about my conversation with Jason until later.

Instead of supporting me and my contention, he walked over to the bed and took up where Jason left off earlier. He held my mom's hand and began telling her about his latest trip to Greece.

"Dear lady, you must come to Greece someday. I will myself take you to see the ancient groves owned by our family's brand of premium olive oil called Lord Papadis."

I listened through one ear until exhaustion claimed me, sleeping about two hours in the recliner, undisturbed, while they talked. By the time visiting hours ended, he was firmly ensconced on Mom's list of conquests, and I was sufficiently rested to wonder where I was going to sleep that night.

Sleep is not what I got, however. Having allowed Mom to convince us she could be left alone with the guards, we were taking our leave when the hospital alarm sounded, sending the entire floor into lockdown. Even with the drapes closed we could see shadows moving in the bright hallway just outside Mom's darkened room.

The police major called in to request entry. "Kincaid's been spotted on the premises by the security cameras. The guard downstairs recognized him, but they weren't able to apprehend him." Turning to Mom she added, "We'll have to rearrange your room as a safety precaution if that's okay, Mrs. Ross."

I could swear my mom enjoyed the whole thing because she smiled and regally nodded her assent. I, however, have never been so frightened in my entire life. This was worse than finding Stella's body and worse than when we found Kincaid in the cove. All I could think about was I brought the danger from Roan Mountain that could destroy everything that had any meaning to me.

It was as dim and mysterious as a cave in our hiding place but far from quiet. Perversely, my mother's energy, undoubtedly aided by some of the drugs she was taking, reasserted itself in the most bizarre way. Instead of lethargic, she grew talkative, chattering about anything and everything to the point one of the guards stuck her head through the curtain and told her to tone it down. Unaccustomed to being spoken to in such an authoritative manner, Mom was inclined to petulance at first but one touch from Christopher's hand calmed her down. The quiet grew obnoxious while we waited in smothering darkness for the twisted mountain man to find us.

Trying not to disturb my mother who was napping, we were quietly puzzling over Kincaid's vendetta against me when she jerked awake. "Mari, what did you call that man? You know, the one who's after you. What's his name?"

Startled, I responded, "It's Jepson Kincaid. He was a ranger on Roan Mountain, but he's turned rogue. Why?"

Clasping her hand over her mouth, my mother stifled an audible gasp. "Cassie knows that man. They're related, maybe cousins!"

I had the strangest feeling a wheel was turning, but I was not in control of the steering.

"It was the oddest thing," she continued. "Cassie showed up at my door without calling one afternoon and said she needed to talk. I was already sick—it was the day before I ended up in the ER—so when she brushed past, me I didn't have the energy to stop her. She was antsy while we spoke, like she was nervous or excited about something, not at all like I remembered her. The jist of the conversation was that a relative from Tennessee—his name was Jep—wanted to come down to visit her. Then she asked me when you would be coming home after all the trouble you'd had on Roan Mountain."

If blood could freeze, mine literally turned to solid ice. They say murderers always leave clues. This one gave advance notice, telling Cassie first, who then casually dropped it into Mom's hands. Now I knew why Kincaid, ever the tracker, found me so easily. He had an inside informant all too ready to help. Before the puzzle pieces locked into place in my mind, Christopher was up and speaking with the guard who immediately radioed her commanding officer.

Coming into the room to stand behind me, he said, "Marianna, if Kincaid shows up, Rambo will protect you like none other. Shall I fetch him?"

"Of course, if the police-major agrees," I told him. I suspected that Rambo was trained in this sort of thing, and now, after the mistreatment he received from Kincaid just a couple of months ago, he had a motive. After yet another whispered conversation, an officer was dispatched and in less than thirty minutes he came up through the staff elevator with both Nell and Rambo in tow.

There was no doubt that my dog was glad to see me, but first he had to greet my mom. Sure of his welcome, he covered her face and hands with numerous licks while she laughed and scratched his ears. Their ritual accomplished, he moved to my side and waited for a signal. He knew something was up and Rambo was ready to roll at my command.

The next hurdle was convincing TPD to let me accompany Rambo through the rabbit warren that was the hospital's inner workings. This feat was not accomplished without serious argument from officers in combat gear who were intent on saving my life.

"You are not trained for this kind of thing, ma'am," police major Younger reminded me with a worried look. "We can't let you do this. Not only could you get killed, but anyone near you will become a target, too."

I could see the reasoning behind their insistence, but chose to stand firm. "You are correct, I'm not trained for this, but my dog is. He'll do even better if I, his handler, accompany him. If I'm willing, I don't see why you shouldn't use me. I've got a big stake in this fight."

With little time to waste, the officer saw my reasoning and had me suited up in body armor while Rambo pawed at the floor, ready to go. I gave him the signal he was waiting for, with Christopher on the other side and members of the TPD flanking us.

The curtains were drawn down the long corridors with all of the doors, elevators, and stairwells locked down. Harsh fluorescent lights, from which little could hide, glowed brittle in the waiting stillness.

Sounds from the gear we wore, the click of Rambo's nails and the subliminal buzz of electronics running in the background were deafening.

Searching for well over an hour, we were nearing a service elevator when Rambo stopped cold. Just ahead pushed close to the wall was an over-sized canvas laundry cart filled with dirty sheets.

Staring straight ahead, ears alert, ridge hair on his back stiff and tail down, Rambo glared at the cart with cold blue eyes.

During that intense fragment of time, the faint imprint of a shoe formed from behind the thick canvas. When it moved just a fraction, Rambo sprang into action. A ghostly apparition with deadly intent, he leaped through the air, the leash flying behind him, to drop into the cart without making a sound.

Up from the unwashed linens came a screaming Jepson Kincaid with Rambo firmly attached to his right hand. A sleek hunting knife clattered to the floor.

When they pulled Kincaid out of the cart, Rambo jumped out and came back to sit by me, a self-satisfied grin on his face. My nemesis, however, was far from finished with us.

"This ain't near about over, bitch!" he cried as they slipped a handcuff onto his good hand. Like a snake covered in oil, he slithered out from underneath the hands that held him. Before anyone could react, Kincaid launched himself at me. Using the metal cuff's loose end as a weapon, he pummeled my head and neck, leaving deep, bloody lacerations.

Literally collapsing to the floor under the force of the attack, my head crashed onto the tiled floor. Almost immediately the metallic taste and scent of my own blood flooded my senses. Within seconds, Rambo attacked with a growl I will never forget, with Christopher right behind him. Together, they lunged onto Kincaid, pushing him off of me.

For once, Rambo was reluctant to give up his prey but at a sharp command from Christopher, he allowed the TPD to drag the rogue ranger away. Kincaid yelled all the way to the elevator and beyond, still cursing at me, but I was too fuzzy to pay attention. Rambo stretched out next to me, refusing to leave my side.

Christopher held my head stable on the floor, cursing under his breath, while doctors and nurses raced toward us. Fading in and out, I felt something calling from a different dimension. I might have answered that call had not Christopher been there.

"My God, what were we thinking?" the police major muttered through gritted teeth. "You're lucky that white shepherd was here or you might have been killed."

"Where is my dog?" I said, mumbling through swelling lips. "Where is Rambo?"

"He's quite the hero, ma'am. He's okay except for some scratches from Kincaid's handcuffs. With your permission, we'd like to take him downtown to our TPD vet for a checkup and a bath." Before she turned away the police major added, "I'll never forget when he leaped through the air like that. It was pure magic. I never saw anything like it before. He moved so fast that it was like watching a ghost fly through the air. We'd love to have him work with us if you'd care to share him."

Ignoring her suggestion, I cried in panic, "Let me see him. Please!" By that time, I was on a gurney and was struggling to breathe, but I had to know for myself that my dog was safe. Not until I felt his warm gritty tongue on my face and over my eyes and mouth was I really certain he was okay. Reaching out to rough up his coat, for the first time I saw the tattoo clearly for what it was—Chi Rho—good fortune, the symbol carved on the support at the cabin where I'd found sanctuary.

Fortunately, the power of morphine to quell pain worked that night, so I slept fairly well. The next morning, seeing the lacerations on my face and neck came as a shock, but I was grateful that's all it was. The body armor had done its job. As a result, Mom and I were both released from the hospital the next day. The spot on her pancreas deemed non-cancerous, and with meds to control future episodes, she was much brighter and more like her old self.

Rambo was moving slowly, as was I, but his injuries were minor and healing fast. Mine took a while longer. Face bruised and swollen, my voice was a rough whisper for weeks, but all in all, I knew we were lucky to be alive.

*****

Shortly after seeing us safely ensconced at Mom's house in Blairstone Forest, Christopher left us to attend a trade show for food and condiment vendors in Orlando.

We were sitting on the back deck talking about Blairstone's community forest when Nell said, "I talked to Saul last night. They've already extradited Jepson to Tennessee. He said word got out and most of the Mountaineers turned out to make sure he was put away properly. He's locked up tight in the Johnson City jail awaiting a court date. It's not likely he'll escape from there. Do you know when Cassie's due to appear before the judge here in Tallahassee?"

A quick check on my smart phone gave me the answer. "Cassie's due to appear before Judge Joannes for a preliminary hearing the day after tomorrow."

Mom paused in the middle of folding a scarf, "Are you planning to attend? Surely you don't want to see Cassie after all the trouble she's caused."

"I'm not going unless a judge tells me I must. If I never see her again it will be too soon."

"Not that you'll find answers at a preliminary hearing, but you might give it a second thought. We still don't know what happened to her or why she's had it in for you. Don't you want to know? I do. I've even wondered if it's something like demonic possession."

"Oh, Mom, I can't believe you of all people would say something like that. Mental illness I can understand but demons? Come on!" Mom and Nell exchanged glances over my head without saying a word. It felt like I had two mothers conspiring against me.

"Come on, you two! I've got nothing to say to her. With her help, that crazy man almost killed me. I've got a hunch she was cheering him on. I don't know why, and I don't care!"

"You'd best think on that tale I told you the day we brought Rambo back from the wild, girl. Your mama might be on to something."

While Nell told the story to my mom, I walked down to the neighborhood lake so that I could think and Rambo could get some exercise. He'd been cooped up for the past several weeks. I knew from experience that some of his latent destructive habits would emerge if he didn't burn that energy off.

Blairstone Forest was developed as the environmental rescue of a highland swamp near downtown Tallahassee. To be in that green place surrounded by trees and close to the water was to retreat from the city's noise. Having gotten accustomed to the natural quiet on Roan Mountain, I found a similar sense of peace in this beautiful place. Best of all, it gave me a place to think about Cassie's betrayal.

In my mind, Cassie's behavior was far more damning than Kincaid's because the animosity he directed at me was there for all to see. Her hatred hurt my heart. In the end, I had to admit that I cared too much about what my best friend had done and that I might not ever understand her real motives.

As it turned out, I had to go to the hearing. Nell volunteered to go with me, so Mom stayed behind with Rambo. She was also packing. We'd received clearance for her to travel, and as soon as Christopher returned, we were going to take her back with us for an extended visit to upper East Tennessee.

The courtroom was crowded as the court had a heavy schedule that day. Reporting on court cases in the past, it never dawned on me that someday I'd be part of one. I watched with apprehension as the prisoners were led in. A couple looked like hardened criminals. One woman looked like a sweet old grannie, two men were well-groomed in contrast with their rumpled orange prison garb, several looked downright dangerous. Then there was Cassie with her carrot-colored hair. All were hand and ankle-cuffed. None maintained eye-contact with the audience.

Cassie's hearing was first on the docket. She looked downcast, and for a full minute, I felt sorry for her until she looked up at me. The sneer which erupted on her face reminded me of a copperhead snake about to strike. Involuntarily, I gasped and drew back, drawing curious stares from those sitting nearby.

"Don't you let that red-headed woman intimidate you, Mari," said Nell with a hiss. "See where she is and what she's got to look forward to, and then look at what you've got."

That got my attention. It was true, I had a lot—a man who loved me, family, friends, a dog named Rambo, and a developing career. When we left the courtroom, I determined to leave my feelings about Cassie behind, but it wasn't that simple. As usual, my emotions rode on my shoulder.

Instead of going straight to Mom's house for lunch, I took Nell to see the converted church where the odyssey with Cassie began. Even though it made me uncomfortable to do it, I pulled into a parking space and stared at the innocuous-looking building. There was nothing about that converted church to indicate what happened that day but it still made me uncomfortable to be there.

"This is the place where Cassie lit up like wildfire in front of my eyes and I saw the madness in her for the first time."

Though she said little, in Nell's comforting presence, the scrim lifted from my eyes. "My God, I see it now. I used to be a mousy little thing Cassie could lead around like a calf with a ring in its nose. She pushed me around like a chess piece, and I usually went where she sent me. Apparently, as long as her authority went unchallenged, we were fine. The worst part is that I didn't even know it was happening! No wonder she got upset when I found Rambo, split with Jason, and got that grant. I wish you could have heard her rant when she heard I was leaving.

The more I thought about it, the more sense it made. "I knew she had roots in Appalachia, but not where. Nor do I recall hearing why her family came to Tallahassee. Getting the residency broke her hold over me here, but not her influence there, because Cassie's first cousin Jepson Kincaid lived in Roan Mountain, Tennessee."

We sat in companionable silence until I said, "I still don't get it. Why should my leaving consume her the way it did? Was it my relationship with Christopher? That doesn't make sense because Jason lived with me and that didn't seem to bother her at all."

"Well, there's no tellin' what she told her cousin about you, girl, but I'm bettin' her feelin's for you were more than friendship, and she felt betrayed," Nell suggested.

I felt the blood drain from my face. "You're kidding," I said, staring hard at her. "Nothing of the sort ever came up between us. Surely I would have sensed something over the years."

"Maybe not. And now, unless she tells you, you'll never know. She may not know herself. It could be none of this would have ever happened if you hadn't stopped for that white dog on the highway and then got the residency. Maybe she couldn't stand the idea of you soaring and leaving her earthbound. About the only thing you can be sure of is that life is a never-ending circle filled with discovery."

*****

The journey to Tennessee with my mom was something I will always treasure. Many years had passed since she'd been to the mountains, and she'd never traveled the great winding highway between Asheville, North Carolina, and Elizabethton, Tennessee. The majesty of the southern highlands, the vivid greens and sky blues kept her in awe and us grinning the entire way. Fortunately, Christopher was driving that stretch because it gave me the opportunity to see her response to the beauty. We laughed and sang at the top of our lungs, and even Rambo caught the contagion, howling while we drove through the mountains.

I was glad it was still daylight when we drove up the eight-mile twisting road to the cabin, because everything she saw delighted my beauty-loving mother. Well, almost everything. "So that's the ranger station where you first met Jepson Kincaid?"

"Yes ma'am, that's the place," I told her. "We'll come down later in the week to meet them. The rangers really are a great bunch. They're still smarting over Kincaid going rogue, and I want to let them know I don't blame them for his behavior."

"Then why don't we bake some cookies and take them when we go?" Mom said. "An offering of food is a great way to mend fences."

I could see the corners of Christopher's mouth twitching. I'd told him earlier that while Mom is a good cook, she can't bake anything without burning it. If my mother saw our communication, she had the grace to ignore it.

"Sure, Mom," I told her, "but we'll have to test the oven first. I haven't baked anything since I got here."

That drew a laugh from Nell. "Sounds like I'd better make plans to come over and help. Ya'll let me know when you commence to bakin', and I'll be on hand to supervise."

When we turned down the gravel track leading down to the cabin, we fell silent.

At the door of the cabin, she paused by the Chi Roe symbol on the porch support, traced it delicately with one finger, and then turned to look at me and Christopher. "Are you sure you want me to stay here? I'd be happy in a Bed & Breakfast nearby."

"No, no, Mrs. Ross, please do not even think of it. We want to share this special place with you," Christopher said. "I've had another bed delivered with extra linens. It's already set up. All you and Marianna have to decide is who gets which bed, unless Rambo makes the decision for you."

Hearing his name, the magical dog who had so changed my life began to prance and whine, his tail wagging like a white flag. He nosed through the partially open front door, pushing into the cabin. By the time we were in, he'd already investigated the place for intruders, deemed it safe, and was asleep on the braided rug in front of the fireplace.

*****

It was June and the mountain laurels were just beginning to bloom when Christopher was again summoned to the olive groves.

"I cannot believe my good fortune to have found you, my love," he told me at the airport in Blountville. "It pains me to leave you, but with Kincaid imprisoned, I must again turn my attention to the family business. I've communicated with Rambo," he added with a grin. "He will be on guard at all times."

Without giving me a chance to respond, heedless of those who watched us, he kissed me deeply, turned, and was gone, virtually disappearing in the security line. Not for the first time, I sensed unbridled passion and wildness in him, or was it other-worldliness? He was made of flesh and blood as I had reason to know, but there was more—he was also a mystery to be unraveled. I looked forward to pulling every thread.

Bereft, I stood alone as travelers rushed past. Feeling restless and unsettled, I climbed the stairs up to the observation platform and watched his plane until it became a mere dot in the sky whispering, "Good fortune, my love, good fortune."

About the Author

Author and professional storyteller Saundra Gerrell Kelley is a native of Tallahassee, Florida. She graduated from Florida State University and later earned an MA in performance art from East Tennessee State University.

Saundra authored *Southern Appalachian Storytellers: Interviews With Sixteen Keepers of the Oral Tradition, Danger in Blackwater Swamp, The Day The Mirror Cried*: a collection of short stories, and now *Danger on Roan Mountain*.

She is an honorary member of the Jonesborough Storytellers Guild where she served as President, and is an Immediate Past President of the Tallahassee Writers Guild.

Follow Saundra Kelley

https://saundrakelley.com/

https://www.facebook.com/AppalachianStorytellers
saundra@saundrakelley.com

www.ingramcontent.com/pod-product-compliance
Lightning Source LLC
Chambersburg PA
CBHW030514260626
47157CB00005B/1738